P

"The feelings r
and

"A witty, wonderfully poised, poignant, self-pityless book."
– *Montreal Gazette*

"Written with exquisite style, perfect pace and unusual
elegance . . . always engaging, it is a genuine tour de force."
– *Hamilton Spectator*

Praise for *Working on Sunday*

"[Phillips] offers diversion, good humour, some entertaining
scenes, a few pungent *aperçus* and a sideways glance
at the human condition." – Carol Shields, *Globe and Mail*

Praise for *The Mice Will Play*

"The writing flows wonderfully . . . . All in all, quite a
lovely read – a pleasure to the eye, the mind, the heart."
– Merilyn Simonds

"A pleasing, light romp reminiscent of an Oscar Wilde
parlour play, with hard truths veiled in happy façades . . . .
Phillips has managed to give his work his own stamp while
reviving a genre – the parlour farce – that's been dormant
for too long." – *Globe and Mail*

"A treat from start to finish . . . . Phillips continues to mine his
rich vein of Wildean wit." – *Quill & Quire*

Buried on Sunday

by Edward O. Phillips

Edward O. Phillips

Buried on Sunday

A Geoffry Chadwick novel

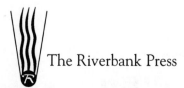

The Riverbank Press

First published in paperback by McClelland & Stewart, 1986
Second publication in hardcover by St. Martin's Press, New York, 1988
Third publication in paperback by The Riverbank Press, 1999

Cover and text design: John Terauds

THE CANADA COUNCIL | LE CONSEIL DES ARTS
FOR THE ARTS | DU CANADA
SINCE 1957 | DEPUIS 1957

We acknowledge the support of the
Canada Council for the Arts for our
publishing program.

Canadian Cataloguing in Publication Data

Phillips, Edward, 1931-
    Buried on Sunday

A Geoffry Chadwick novel.
ISBN 1-896332-12-9

I. Title.

PS8581.H567B87 1999   C813'.54   C99-931414-9
PR9199.3.P44B87 1999

The Riverbank Press
P.O. Box 456, 31 Adelaide St. East, Toronto, Ontario, Canada M5C 2J5

Printed and bound in Canada by Métrolitho

for E.J.S
K.S.W.

Solomon Grundy,
Born on Monday,
Christened on Tuesday,
Married on Wednesday,
Took ill on Thursday,
Worse on Friday,
Died on Saturday,
Buried on Sunday.
This is the end
Of Solomon Grundy.

Anon.

I

I have always detested wine and cheese parties. If heaven, perish the thought, is a place of milk and honey, then hell must be an abode of wine and cheese. Imagine an eternity of heartburn brought on by sipping those questionable vintages which come in brown glass gallon jugs while one chooses between air-dried cheddar or leaky Brie whose rind tastes of ammonia. The question might logically arise as to why I found myself almost prepared to drink a naïve white wine, totally without breeding or presumption, and to balance an unco-operative chunk of feta on a disintegrating cracker.

> *Wheat Thins, Triscuits, wheel of Brie,*
> *Keep the bores away from me.*

The reason was simple: it was Sunday afternoon. I am convinced that God invented Sunday not so that we might rest but to remind us weekly just how meagre our inner resources really are. For a single man who has spilled over into his fifties, Sundays can be trying, especially the afternoons. I am now fifty-three years old, far from dead I hasten to add, not even world-weary – a rather self-conscious attitude, I have always thought. Still, the inescapable fact remains that after half a century there are few surprises, least of all emotional ones. Furthermore, one has learned to weigh pleasures against penalties; a night on the town is seldom worth the following day's hangover. It is no longer fun to wake up beside a stranger and be obliged to offer him breakfast, particularly when one has had about three hours' sleep. When I die and go to heaven, as Mother used to say about dead friends and relatives, I hope I will be buried on Sunday, my last, silent protest against this hideously dreary day.

To be middle aged is to belong to a club whose dues are twinges of arthritis first thing upon arising, a tendency towards insomnia, a bottle of Rolaids in the medicine cabinet, in case one forgets and eats cooked tomatoes in any form. Dues often take the form of *déjà vu*, in novels begun and never finished, television programs switched off, conversations with the young who tell you with bright-eyed solemnity all about themselves. Dues can be as simple as realizing the idea of a party is always more enjoyable than the party itself, as knowing Florence and Siena can never again be seen with the clear unspoiled eye of a student, as accepting the unfortunate but axiomatic truth that once a love affair has ended there is no going back. A point which has again been proven.

Yesterday morning I was weighing the pros and cons of a third cup of black coffee on an empty stomach when the telephone rang. I reached for the receiver, wondering whether something unforeseen had come up which would oblige me to go down to the office, and hoping it wasn't. The voice was totally unexpected, belonging to someone I knew to be living in Vancouver who had given me no warning of his intention to come east. He claimed to have come to Montreal on business, that all-purpose word which covers a multitude of shenanigans. Nor was he specific as to the nature of his business. It was a short visit, a couple of days maximum, and he did admit that one of his reasons for coming to Quebec was to see me. He suggested lunch; he wanted to take me out. I suggested he drop by my apartment for a drink first. We agreed on noon, and hung up.

I went into the bathroom and began the task of making myself presentable. (I may be shop-worn but my underwear is always clean.) Faced with the problem of what to put on, a suit being too formal, a sweater perhaps too casual, I compromised on a jacket and light-grey flannels. A tie still takes you anywhere.

By the time I had finished dressing I had nothing to do but wait for Chris to arrive. I do not as a rule ask people up to my apartment, for a number of reasons. To begin with, there is a doorman, one of those super-discreet lackeys who hide behind a navy-blue suit and a middle-European accent. Self-effacing to the point of invisibility (*only the Shadow knows*), I'll bet he could come up with more dirt on the residents in the building than the RCMP. I like to keep him guessing.

Some people look on their apartments as home, the place where their better self is free to emerge. Others see their flats as nests and line them with the human equivalent of twigs and string: photographs, souvenirs, white elephants from garage sales and church bazaars, which the devil made them buy. Still others see their houses or apartments as an extension of their profession or craft, and live in a welter of paints, brushes, clay, armatures, remnants, books, and newspaper clippings. Last, and probably least, are those who look upon their apartments as lairs, places in which to retreat and exclude the world, not invite it it. I have always subscribed to the lair school of homemaking, the desire to keep the world at bay becoming more pronounced with each successive birthday.

My apartment is furnished with traditional but excellent taste for which much of the credit must go to my mother, who made hanging out at auctions into something of a career. The

prevailing colours of sienna and ochre are highlighted by a few
bits of silver, which my current cleaning woman loves to buff
with a rouge cloth while humming hymns. Two Corinthian
candlesticks keep one another company on the small oak table
I use for eating, while a Paul Revere bowl on the walnut coffeetable holds book matches pinched from restaurants even though
I don't smoke. Off by itself in a corner of the living room,
positioned by the window with the view, sits a Charles Eames
chair with matching footstool.

There had been a time when Chris was a regular visitor to
my apartment, his visits prearranged, his arrival always
punctual. As I waited yesterday morning, I realized there was
something uncharacteristic about the last-minute quality of his
call. I stood staring out the window in a kind of semi-trance.
Had the building across the street exploded I would probably
not have noticed.

For some years, I had loved Christopher Pratt with a single-
mindedness that surprised even me. I did not have to count the
ways. He occupied my entire consciousness, front and centre,
with a follow spot. Not that I hadn't been in love before. Without resorting to Ecclesiastes, there is a time for being in love.
When one is young the condition of love is as natural as
breathing. But not as a rule at fifty. By the time one has clocked
up half a century, being in love is not a condition but an affliction.

He was a married man with children, assistant headmaster of
a highly respected private school, the kind of man who used to
be called a pillar of the community. I applauded the fact that
he and his wife did not have one of those tacky arrangements
known as open marriage. Consequently our own love affair was
clandestine, our meetings on the sly, our moments of happiness

or passion or communion snatched from that middle-aged schedule which sees accounted for every moment from day-break to moonrise. And yet so profound was my intoxication there was a time when I actually allowed myself to believe Chris and I might spend our old age together.

Ours had not been a dramatic break-up, operatic gestures and final exit, stage left, but rather more of a winding down. The saddest part of the story, perhaps I should say ironic, was that only after Chris and I had separated did he divorce his wife, quit his job, and eventually move out to the west coast, ostensibly to study for a Ph.D. It was a case of male menopause at its most marked. The unexpected call had been the first communication since his departure two years ago, and it was with some trepidation that I looked forward to seeing him.

Now as I stood at my living room window, thinking about Chris and our time together the previous day, I have to confess I was also thinking about the highball my commonsense told me was too early in the afternoon to pour. At half-past four on a wet Sunday afternoon one should get drunk, get laid, or commit suicide. It is no time to begin reading Proust.

"Geoffry darling!" I could still hear Madeleine's voice. "You are the most difficult man to reach. I've been calling and calling. This Sunday afternoon: a few people in for wine and cheese. My sister's over for a visit, the one who lives in Bath. I've told her I'm inviting the most attractive man in Westmount. You must come, even if it's only for an hour. Now I won't take no for an answer. Five o'clock on. Oh, and dress casual. *Très en famille.*"

She had called me at my office earlier in the week and insisted on being put through, obliging the client, who was paying for my legal advice, to study his fingernails in elaborate

pantomime of pretending not to listen. Women like Madeleine
have an enormous capacity for getting their own way. When a
Sherman tank comes lumbering down the road you can do one
of three things: stand still and allow yourself to be squashed
flat, step aside, or blow it up. I prefer to step aside. I muttered
something about doing my best to make it and hung up.
Naturally I had no intention of turning up. I recalled the last
time I had gone to Madeleine's house, an endless brunch at
which I found myself seated between an unpublished poet, who
had just run her first marathon, and a social worker who was
studying Russian.

But here I stood on this grey Sunday afternoon, still in my
bathrobe, unwashed, unshaved, uncombed, the weekend papers
in drifts across the carpet. My mood matched my appearance.
There were no movies I really wanted to see, and I was holding
out against the one about that little lost creature from outer space.
From what I can gather it is an expensive remake of *Lassie
Come Home*.

What the hell, I decided on impulse. Why not pull myself
together and meet the sister from Bath. *Faute de mieux*. I
showered, shaved, dressed, pulling on an old tweed jacket from
the innermost reaches of my closet. The suede patches on the
elbows were themselves a kind of silent protest.

I decided to leave my car and walk up the hill to Madeleine's. The spring air was filled with an almost tactile softness.
The rain had ended. So had something between Chris and me.

When I'd opened the door to him yesterday, I found him
changed, and not for the better. Formerly a conservative dresser,
he now turned up wearing a khaki leisure suit. The short, well-
trimmed hair I remembered now bloomed around his head in a

luxuriant Afro aureole. In place of a tie, a braided leather bola around his neck supported a large chunk of turquoise. He wore jogging shoes in shades of psychedelic blue. What was worse, his attitudes had changed along with his appearance.

We exchanged the usual platitudes about health and major activities as I pulled the cork on a bottle of white wine. Before Chris had even taken a sip he pulled out a box of cigarette papers, a plastic bag half-filled with something that looked like catnip, and rolled himself a joint. Although I grew up during a time when everyone else seemed to puff away, I am a non-smoker. And unlike a heavy smoker who has stopped, I am not militant about other people's cigarettes. However I do have two objections to marijuana. It turns the user remote, or silly, or both. The odour is immensely disagreeable, like French cigarettes, only worse.

By the time he had roach-clipped his way through a joint and a half, I felt as though we were conversing under water, an impression lunch did nothing to dispel. Furthermore, I was quite dismayed at how little residue there seemed to be of our years together. In the exposed environment of a public restaurant, I came to the full realization of what I had begun to suspect back in my apartment. Chris and I really had nothing to say to one another. Our lives had diverged; we no longer shared the same city, community, concerns, when each day's events could be discussed at length. For most adults, a return to graduate school results less from a desire to pursue learning than from an attempt to recapture youth, at least those golden years of college. It is a regression, one of the duller ones. And like certain types of wine, corporate law does not travel well, at least not outside the office. What interests me about my work is of scant interest to others.

I did not find myself in the least curious about Chris's newly acquired, free-form, west-coast lifestyle. It was evident to me, without glossary or footnotes, that Chris had embraced soft drugs, casual sex, and the attendant absence of routine which regards deadlines and engagement calendars as useless baggage.

I was also beginning to pick up intimations, or vibes. Between joints and his fair share of the two litres of wine we had already polished off, Chris was mellowing out. (Something about the mere smell of marijuana does something spacy to my vocabulary.) I wasn't absolutely certain about what was on whatever was left of his mind; but my guess was, speaking in heraldic terms, that it had to do with Chadwick, couchant, on a bed, Simmons.

By way of throwing some conversational landfill into the long, swampy pauses, which bothered me far more than they appeared to bother Chris, I asked where he was staying and when he intended to leave Montreal. He replied that he was "loose," that he had no place to stay at the moment, that he had hoped he might "crash" on my couch.

At once my radar began to beep. I knew how unlikely it would be for Chris to spend the night on the sofa. And, I must confess, the idea of sleeping with him did not repel me. Once more wasn't going to make that much difference. But I found myself hesitating. Chris was not one of those friends with whom sex can be casual and uncomplicated. Chris had been my lover, a man whose spirit as well as his skin had touched mine. To sleep with him would be a regression, like his return to graduate school. Maybe I was reluctant to tamper with the past, to risk tarnishing a memory that for all its difficulties I still wanted to cherish. In my gut I knew renewing that kind of intimacy with Chris would be a mistake.

I suggested that he would not be the least bit comfortable on my couch and that I would be glad to put him up at a hotel. We shadowboxed verbally, but I held firm. Once the idea managed to filter through the cannabis and the Chablis that he was not going to spend the night in my apartment, he announced his decision to return to Vancouver that afternoon. I offered to drive him to the airport. All he had in the way of luggage was a shoulder bag, which he had brought with him to the restaurant. After he paid the bill we walked directly to the garage under my apartment building.

We did not speak on the way to the airport. Somehow silence seemed more comfortable than conversation by the yard. I drove up the departure ramp. Chris got out. He gave me his telephone number in Vancouver. We muttered the standard lines: Thanks. Don't mention it. Take care. See you next time around. Let me know when you come out west. Have a safe trip. So long. And he was absorbed into the concourse, out of sight, unfortunately not out of mind.

I drove home slowly. Saying goodbye to Chris was like saying goodbye to my forties all over again. I realized with dismay I no longer even much liked the man whom I had once loved, and I found myself prey to intimations of mortality and assaulted by all those thoughts that do often lie too deep for tears.

But regrets, in particular those for events long since past, are ultimately a waste of time and energy. The snows of yesteryear have melted. Or, as my mother would say, "There is no use crying over spilled milk." (Of course she never touches milk, spilled or otherwise, and saves her tears for spilled vodka, which she now drinks, instead of gin.) She might even have suggested that he travels fastest who travels alone, a bit of folk wisdom rendered obsolete by the jet plane. I was indeed travelling alone, although at the moment I had no place to go except Madeleine's house. Falling back on a coinage of my own, that emphysema is better than no breath at all, I continued to direct my leisurely steps towards a destination I was in no particular hurry to reach.

After the climb up the hill, I was walking up the flagstone path leading to the large stone house in Upper Westmount. I rang the softly glowing doorbell. As Madeleine opened the door and swept me inside I could see she had pulled a switcheroo, telling the guests to dress casually so she would look all the more resplendent in tangerine silk and pearls. Women who are built to last, like Madeleine, ought not to wear warm colours. She brought to mind a soft-drink dispenser.

It was not difficult to spot the sister from Bath, pleated plaid skirt with one of those enormous diaper pins in front, and teased hair. She had beefy British hands and her grip was a real knuckle-grinder. Most of the other guests I had met; they belonged to Madeleine's troupe of strolling players. Our common bond, if such it could be called, was the awareness we had showed up at Madeleine's gathering in order to stave off the Sunday afternoon sinker. I said hello to an antique dealer and his friend, a strapping six-footer who designs children's clothes. Madeleine believes that belonging to a minority group automatically makes one interesting. For her there are no boring hairdressers.

After I had run the gauntlet of introductions, Madeleine tucked my arm firmly between her left arm and left breast and steered me into the dining room where the teak sideboard had been set up as a bar, and the dining room table as buffet.

Displayed on platters and in baskets was an overkill assortment of cheeses, biscuits, breads, along with a large bowl of hummus, the peanut butter of the intelligentsia. Had I a penchant for metaphor I might have said the board groaned, although teak tends to creak.

Madeleine belongs to that group of women who would never dream of having a decorator help pull the house together. To engage an interior designer would be equivalent to admitting one had no taste. Women of Madeleine's generation believe they were born with good taste, the way all men of the same vintage believe they have a sense of humour. Madeleine had dealt with the house by turning her back on the Scottish baronial look which informs most of her community. The house is vaguely comtemporary, as opposed to modern. Her friends drink a lot; after a while they ignore coasters and set down onto the bare wood tumblers coated with condensation. Madeleine's retirement project will be getting the rings off her teak furniture.

In the dining room she has eschewed paintings in favour of wall hangings which celebrate the warp and the weft in wool, string, sisal. Madeleine herself dabbles in weaving; and, like most amateurs, takes disproportiate pride in her work which she displays prominently. Her bibelots, or objects of art, run heavily to museum reproductions. Bastet, the Egyptian cat goddess wearing electroplated gold earrings, dominates the mantel and is flanked by candlesticks whose bases are dolphins with their bodies twisted into an unlikely S-curve. A plump, placid Buddah squats on the coffeetable, while on the bookshelf in the front hall stands a foot-high reproduction of Michelangelo's *David*, his tiny bronze appendage shiny from being rubbed by tipsy guests.

"So you're the most attractive man in Westmount!" boomed a voice at my elbow. I turned to confront the visiting sister.

"If you're unlucky enough to like the type," I replied as I noticed with dismay that her left hand was innocent of a wedding ring.

Her reply was a bray of mirth, a laugh filled with field-hockey sticks and bloomers. She had the ankles to match. I could easily imagine her taking a tramp on the Broads.

"Did you have a good flight across the Atlantic?" I continued, paying my dues as guest.

"Spotty. Smooth sailing, but the stewardess was a bit uppity. I asked for a slice of lemon for my tea and she replied she had heaps off other passengers to serve. Spilled a blood Mary down the front of her uniform. Served her bloody well right. I was in tucks."

"There you are, Alice!" exclaimed Madeleine as she unfurled herself into the dining room, pearls sledding down her chest and plunging into a void. "Come and meet the Bradys. They're driving us up to the Laurentians for lunch next week." And she bore her sister away, to my immense relief.

"See you later," said the sister archly over her shoulder. I had a feeling I would have discovered far more in common with that movie creature from outer space than with this caryatid from the U.K.

A woman came into the dining room, tall, blonde, wearing the classic Chanel suit. Seeing me, she stopped short and smiled. "Geoffry, Geoffry Chadwick. How wonderful to see you after all this time."

I was taken by surprise. Some moments passed before the coin dropped. "Catherine Bradford!" We shook hands in that uncertain way of people wondering whether they should exchange the ritual social kiss. "And what have you been doing for the last twenty-five years?"

"In twenty-five words or less?" She released my hand from the firm grasp she had given it. "I got married, moved to Ontario, raised a family, became a widow, married a second time and resumed my maiden name. How many words is that?"

We laughed. "Would I be impolite to presume the second husband is younger than you?"

"What makes you say that?" She smiled in anticipation of my reply.

"You have become a blonde. A woman generally becomes a blonde because there is no man in her life, or there is and he is younger."

"That sounds suspiciously like a *perçu*, or a bit of folk wisdom told you by an old gypsy fortune-teller after you had crossed her palm with silver. But the provoking thing is that you are right." She smiled. "But then you always were provoking, Geoffry, even as a young man. I realize now you must have been just as insecure as the rest of us, only you were much more adroit at concealing it. I am glad to see you again. Tell me honestly. Do you like the hair? Does it make me look cheap and approachable?" She ran a manicured hand over her short pageboy.

"Eminently, but I like it. I miss the stick barette with two lovebirds, but I still like it. Every woman should be a blonde at least once during her lifetime. At least you don't have bangs. A woman who wears bangs looks as though she should come padding into the room with slippers in her mouth."

Catherine laughed out loud. I suppose I could have called

her laugh infectious, but I save that stale figure of speech for my sister Mildred, especially when she has her annual autumn cold.

"Am I to meet number-two husband?"

"Not tonight. He's in the country."

"What a shame. I am always more curious about second husbands than first ones. Women who are foolhardy enough to marry a second time generally do so for companionship or a tax shelter. Which was yours?"

"Companionship, I suppose. I think I am his tax shelter. And although I blush to admit it, when we interface he's very user friendly."

"Why should you blush? You are certainly old enough to know better, and obviously you do. I am certain you were taught as a girl that being a lady was a question of appetite: little for food and none for sex. I, on the other hand, was brought up to be a gentleman: do anything, anything at all, but don't talk about it. Now it would appear ladies do everything, and talk about it. And that is just what I want you to do. Let's hide in the breakfast nook and you can tell me how you were swept off your feet."

Madeleine's house came equipped with a small maid's room off the kitchen, which she had turned into an eating nook. The room served as a reminder of the time when servants were truly oppressed, working long hours with only Thursday afternoons and every other Sunday off. Nowadays no self-respecting maid would put up with a cubbyhole off the kitchen. Madeleine's maid, a surly Jamaican, inhabits a suite of rooms in the finished basement complete with colour TV.

Catherine and I settled ourselves on straight-backed chairs with quilted seat pads and prepared to catch up on two and one half decades.

I had known Catherine Bradford for a long time, although never very well. She was my wife's cousin and maid of honour at our wedding all those many years ago. Shortly after Susan and our daughter were killed in the crash, Catherine herself married and moved away from Montreal.

As I sat across the table from this poised and beautiful woman, I could scarcely remember the plump, auburn-haired, somewhat amorphous young woman who had preceeded Susan and me down the aisle. What I remembered best was her laugh, hearty and spontaneous, almost unladylike according to the tenets of her upbringing. The only time I had met her first husband was at the wedding. Most weddings spotlight the bride; the groom does little more than a walk-on cameo. I can scarcely remember him, clean-cut, good-looking, in that die-stamped way. Catherine and I were always going to get together, but Hamilton was not on my beat. After a while even the Christmas cards petered out. And now she had materialized at Madeleine's wine and cheese rout.

"You've changed," I found myself saying with no great originality. "And for the better. You're older, but at the same time less matronly than I remember."

"That's good to hear. When I was twenty I aspired to being a matron. I really wanted the children, the stroller, the washing machine. But I've turned in my motherhood badge. I enjoyed the experience, but now I've done with it."

"Do you like your children?"

She did not seem in the least surprised by the question. "As a matter of fact yes, very much. My daughter is married with a baby on the way. And my son is so good-looking it really doesn't matter that he's not very bright." She smiled. "I suppose that's not quite fair. I guess he's intelligent enough, but he's terribly keen on sports. And just between these four walls, Geoffry, I have always secretly believed men who play games after the age of twenty-one are not very smart."

"Funny you should say that," I replied in a tone of voice which said clearly I agreed with her. I remembered hearing through the grapevine that her first husband had died on the squash court. The heart of gold he was reported to have had turned out to be made of baser metal. "It has been my experience that men who play games usually end up married to women who do their own decorating. How would you describe this room, interesting or different?"

"Neither." She studied the yellow and white painted furniture, the polka-dot net curtains, the gingham dog and calico cat battling their way across the wallpaper. "But if you locked me in here for an hour or so I'd be willing to confess to anything: murder, treason, shoplifting." She smiled a smile which etched lines into her face. Far from disfiguring, the lines heightened her beauty, outlining the planes and contours which had begun to emerge with age.

About certain men I know it has been said they have a taste for women, meaning they are constantly on the make. To have a taste for anything requires distance and perspective, and that includes women as well. At the risk of sounding like an apologist, I have always believed the discriminating homosexual has far more appreciation of beautiful women than the macho moron who is constantly chinning himself on his own sexuality.

For a moment I was tempted to explain why I had not written to Catherine when her first husband died, but I reconsidered. Why make a clumsy apology for something I failed to do ten years ago. Let sleeping dogs, especially gingham ones, lie.

Out of sight, but not out of earshot, we heard Madeleine invade the kicthen to deal with the maid. "Isolene, cut more French bread and make the slices thinner this time. We're nearly out of Triscuits, and the Brie looks terribly mauled. Bring a fresh slice."

The sound of wine being decanted into a jug reminded me that both Catherine and I faced empty glasses. "Catherine, I have a splendid idea. Since you are a grass widow why not have dinner with me? I will not lay siege to your virtue. I would like company. Besides, you'll be doing me a favour. Let me take you away from all this."

"To the clean, pure life I've always wanted? I have to confess I'm very tempted, but I'm sorry to say I promised to have dinner with Father. I stay with him when I'm in the city."

"You're not back living in Montreal, then."

"No, we moved to the country shortly after we returned to Quebec. My husband is in real estate, and selling country property from an office in Montreal meant a lot of travelling. Living in the country was a logical solution."

"Don't you miss the bright lights and the dry cleaners?"

"At times. But I get into town quite often. And I have friends out to stay. It's a beautiful spot, right on Lake Memphremagog." She paused for a moment. "Geoffry, next weekend is the twenty-fourth of May and a long holiday weekend. If you have no other plans, why not come out and spend it with us?"

I guess the look of dismay was easy to decode. I had no plans for the upcoming weekend, other than dinner with Mother. But weekend house parties in the country are far more interesting to read about than to experience, and I have an aversion to being a houseguest.

Catherine smiled. "Now before you begin inventing alibis, let me assure you of your own room and bath. No bunk beds, no sleeping bags, no dormitories, no standing in line for the toilet. I have plenty of sheets and blankets, the towels are not transparent, and I did not furnish the house with things I no longer needed in the city."

" 'When one is in town one amuses oneself. When one is in the country one amuses other people. It is excessively boring.' I rest my case with Oscar Wilde."

"But, Geoffry, we will all be there to entertain you; or, better yet, to help you entertain yourself. How can you possibly not come?"

"Catherine, the truth shall set us free: I am a bad houseguest, cranky, demanding, ungrateful. My idea of roughing it is to complain about room service. I feel in all honour I must refuse."

Catherine clapped her hands together in appreciation. "After all that, I wouldn't dream of letting you refuse. I owe it to my honour as a hostess to accept the Chadwick challenge, *le défi* Chadwick, as we say in the Townships. I shall expect you on Friday, any time after lunch."

The truth quite obviously does not set us free. "There's something else. The country is filled with spiders – not literary ones such as Miss Muffet encountered or kindly Charlotte of the web, but real ones, hairy, horrendous, and every last one of them out to get me."

"Well, if you ever find yourself trapped by a spider all you have to do is whistle. 'You know how to whistle, don't you? You just put your lips together . . .' "

" ' . . . and blow.' Catherine, I will accept your invitation on one condition."

"What's that?"

"That you help me to escape from the visiting sister, for whom I believe I have been laid on. Pretend I am taking you out to dinner and that it was already agreed on before we arrived. We'll have enough trouble prying ourselves loose from Madeleine."

As anticipated, our hostess practically threw her orange body across the doorway to prevent us from leaving, insisting that we'd only just arrived, that the three of us hadn't had a chance to chat, that we hadn't even touched the cheese, that more guests were still due, and that her nephew had promised to play some Chopin even though the piano was hideously out of tune.

"You did say, 'If only for an hour,' " I reminded her. "And Catherine and I are in rather a hurry to slide into sin. It's been lovely, Madeleine. Thanks."

Above our heads the doorbell rang. A fresh surge of guests forced Madeleine to give ground, allowing Catherine and me to make good our escape. Catherine drove me home, and gave me her phone number in the country, promising to put a map in the mail tomorrow. I jotted my address on the back of my business card.

The evening was still young when I let myself into my apartment. The idea came suddenly to mind that it was mid-afternoon on the west coast and that Chris had given me a number where he might be reached. I thought about calling him, not that I had anything important to say. But I was nagged by the uncomfortable feeling that I failed to answer some kind of S.O.S. Should I have taken a softer line with him, or expressed more interest in his life of late? In my attempt at self-preservation perhaps I had been unnecessarily abrupt and dismissive. "Reach out and touch," goes the popular slogan. I had failed to do either; and a casual phone call, a simple "Hello, just thinking of you," certainly couldn't do any harm.

I dialled. The phone rang three times before a totally unfamiliar voice answered. "Pratt residence."

Across the long distance wire came the sound of muffled whispers, muted giggles. Then Chris came onto the line. "Yes?"

"Sorry to interrupt the tutorial, but I was curious as to whether you got back in one piece."

"Geoffry! You're the last person I expected to call."

"Evidently. I hope it wasn't a case of coitus interruptus," I said with a sardonic edge I made no effort to conceal.

"No, no. Just one of those things."

"A trip to the moon on gossamer wings?"

"Not exactly. Is anything wrong?"

"No. I was just checking in. Now I'll check out and let you get back to your research." And so the conversation ended.

Why are we, like velcro, always so reluctant to let go? For some reason I could not clearly explain it bothered me to think of Chris in bed with someone else. To know in the abstract he had been running around was not like hearing a stranger's voice on the bedroom phone. I did not wish I was there; I could not blame my feeling on jealousy, sexual or otherwise. Perhaps what saddened me was the confirmation of how totally our relationship had ended. I found myself thinking of my wife Susan in a way I had not thought of her in years. That relationship too had ended. But the cause had been external, a runaway truck on a steep incline. I still loved the woman who had been killed. Death removed the object but not the emotion. In spite of all the people I had known since, I have never stopped loving Susan. I guess I never will.

But Chris was a different story. Like a high school English teacher giving a class on the short story, I could point out a beginning, a middle, and an end.

My memory was clearly acting up, like an elbow aching from an old sports injury. Nothing pushes the past back where it belongs more effectively than the intense if empty nowness of the television screen. After pouring myself a drink I pushed the On button. During the first commercial break I telephoned for barbecued chicken. I had eaten nothing at the party. My growling stomach was a futher reminder of how much life is lived in the present.

II

Every Monday morning I am seized with a distinct reluctance to get out of bed. On this particular morning the alarm clock, which I had taken the precaution to set, bullied me into consciousness, pulling me from the depths of a middle-weight nightmare. The dream was vague, but it had to do with being marooned in a country cottage with only an outhouse and a cold-water hand pump.

By ten minutes to eight I had ingested coffee and the morning paper. The telephone began to ring. When someone gets around to updating Dante, making him more relevant for the post-Me Generation, I want him to put Alexander Graham Bell right down there in the ninth circle along with Judas, Brutus, and Cassius. The telephone is an instrument of the devil, but between the demands of clients and those of an accident-prone mother, I feel compelled to answer.

The telephone on the kitchen wall continued to hector me, and I picked up the receiver. "Yes?"

"Geoffry? Is that you?" My sister's voice is as shattering glass or clashing cymbal.

"You were expecting maybe the Emperor Shapiro-Hito?"

"It's Mildred. Your voice sounded odd."

"You are hearing the first words I have spoken this morning."

"I see. How is Mother?"

"Terrific. She's on the wagon; she's stopped chain-smoking; she jogs five miles a day; and she's taking a course in cabinet-making."

"You're not the least bit funny, Geoffry. You know how worried I am."

"Sure I know. That's why you're holed up in Toronto. She has given up gin for vodka; she has taken to smoking low-tar cigarettes; and her limp is less noticeable. Unfortunately, however, it will disqualify her from the Miss Teen Canada contest."

A snort of impatience came over the line.

"Mildred, some things never change. You might just as well ask me how is Mount Everest, or how are the ruins at Chichen Itza. Mother is the same as she always was, permanently out-of-focus. In a world racked by mutability, Mother and the *Winged Victory* do not change."

"Is she eating properly?"

"She uses a knife and fork, very prettily too, I might add. And she always wipes her mouth on a napkin between bites."

"Nutrition! I am talking about nutrition."

"She's alive, isn't she? Madame is still shovelling truck driver meals onto the table and Mother is still pecking away. What more can I say?" I was just about to announce I was in a terrible hurry and hang up.

"Geoffry – " her voice went flutey-fluttery, so I knew we were coming to the real reason for the call – "Elizabeth is coming up to Montreal for a few days . . . "

"No! She cannot stay with me. I have only one bedroom and I do not intend to have her camping out on the couch."

"You won't have to. She is going to stay with Mother. But I was hoping you'd keep an eye on her."

"You mean chaperon? I make a lousy duenna. My hair is too short to hold a Spanish comb, and I trip over the mantilla."

"You're being very tiresome. All I want you to do is to – to behave like an uncle for once. Tell her what to do, what to see, and where not to go."

"Why is she coming up?"

"To audition. She has decided she wants to be a singer, and there is an outstanding teacher in Montreal."

"Isn't she a bit scrawny to be a singer?"

"You'd be surprised at how she has filled out. That is if you ever took the trouble to notice your nieces."

"Mildred, men of my age who notice girls of Elizabeth's age go to prison. When is she coming up?"

"Today, on the eleven o'clock train."

"Have her call me when she gets to Mother's. I'll buy her some lunch and tell her not to get into cars with strange men. Does she have any personal peculiarities? Green hair? Safety pins in her ears? Does she burst unprovoked into song like Grace Moore or Deanna Durbin in those movie musicals we love to hate?"

"Indeed not. My daughter is a lady."

"Tell her to call. And now I must go. My first appointment is at nine. I have to sluice. This is not *au revoir*; it is goodbye."

It has occurred to me more than once that were Mildred my daughter and not my sister, I would not have asked myself, "Where did I go wrong?" but, "Is there anything I did right?" But what can you expect of a woman who has saved every single Christmas card she has ever received since she was married?

I am not so naïve as to believe every day should soar, but some days never seem to make it off the ground. To begin the day with a phone call from my sister was already an omen, like bad news from the sheep's entrails.

I arrived at my office to be brought up sharply by the reminder that my secretary had gone on vacation; an apparition from Substitute Secretaries occupied her desk. Hair of uniform colour and sheen lay across her head in Little Orphan Annie curls. Few women can get away with *décolletage*; no woman can get away with *décolletage* at the office. If the secret was in the circle, as the ads suggest, it was an ill-kept secret. At the end of a long chain hung a head of Nefertiti in profile. A blue Mary medal dangled from her watch band. I did not even have to look to know she wore an ankle bracelet. I expect a secretary to look like a secretary, not like the night teller in a sperm bank.

As I crossed the reception area she looked up from her *People* magazine and smiled. "Are you Mr. Chadwick? I'm Gladys Walker. I'm replacing Mrs. Patterson while she's on vacation."

"I see. Very well, Miss Walker. Can you handle a dictaphone?"

"Yes, sir."

"I will have some letters for you presently. When my first appointment turns up please show him in."

I waited until half-past nine, a civilized hour, then telephoned Catherine at her father's apartment to say my niece was coming unexpectedly to town, and I would have to squire her around over the long weekend, and I would be unable to come to the country. I really was very sorry as I had so been looking forward to it. I am only a moderately good liar. As a propitiary offering I volunteered to buy her some lunch today before she returned to the country.

She accepted with what sounded like obvious pleasure and I suggested she pick me up at my office at noon. The other partners in the law firm of Lyall, Pierce, Chadwick, and Dawson are worthy men all; but, like Highway 401 to Toronto, straight and boring. Having a beautiful woman collect me for lunch wouldn't hurt my image one bit.

I had hardly hung up the telephone when the red light began to flicker. I picked up the receiver.

"Your wife is on the line," announced Galdys Walker in a slightly aggrieved tone.

"I have no wife, Miss Walker."

"She said it was Mrs. Chadwick," she answered cheerfully.

"It is my mother. Please put her through."

"Yes, sir."

I waited a moment for Mother to come onto the line.

"Geoffry?" she asked tentatively, almost as if she did not really expect me to materialize on the other end of the wire.

"Mother. This is an unusual hour for you to call. Is anything wrong?"

"Why should anything be wrong?"

I let the question go by. If I had tried to chronicle the list of potential disasters Mother could precipitate, it would take at least half an hour. "Oh, nothing," I replied. "Just a figure of speech. Did you sleep well?"

"As a matter of fact, yes. Madame made a lovely soufflé for supper and we ate in front of the television set. We watched "Fraggle Rock." It was so amusing. One of the Fraggles, I can't remember which, didn't know what he wanted to do with his life, so he went to consult Marjory the trash heap. Really, Geoffry, she is nothing but a pile of garden cuttings, but she comes to life and carries a lorgnette and talks in the most comical fashion."

"Mother, I hate to seem rude, but I have clients waiting. What was it you wanted to say?"

"What was it now? Oh, yes. Your sister Mildred telephoned to say Elizabeth is coming to town today. Will you come for dinner? I've invited Walter."

"Sure thing, Mother. I'll be there around seven. Now I must go."

"Geoffry?"

"Yes, Mother?" I tried to keep the impatience out of my voice.

"I wanted to ask you something, but now I can't seem to re-member what it is." There followed a pause, one of those irritating pauses, like waiting for Alka-Seltzer to dissolve. "Never mind, I'll ask you this evening."

"When you think of it again, write it down. Bye, now." I hung up before she strayed into another byway. People who fill their days with nothing in particular never want to get off the tele-phone.

I spent most of the morning turning a private citizen into a private corporation. He and his accountant seemed to think a real tax benefit would follow. The scheme failed to convice me; all it appeared to accomplish was to defer tax, not avoid it. However, I was not being paid for an opinion but for an incor-poration. My client was a self-made man, full of admiration for his creator. He had a face full of expense account living and tassels on his loafers – and views, on everything. It was a long morning, and I consequently felt relief when the red light on my phone began to flicker, and Miss Walker announced a Mrs. Bradford waited in the foyer.

It was with no little amusement that I watched Gladys Walker studying Catherine Bradford as she greeted me. To use a forties expression, Catherine looked stunning. If her style leaned toward *Town and Country*, she knew how to carry it off. The fragrance of money rose from her Italian handbag and shoes. (A glimpse of shoes can tell me volumes about the wearer.)

Just recently I had learned of a new Italian restaurant, Trattoria di Parma, one of those discoveries about which people tell you only after swearing you to secrecy. Such restaurants generally have a short life span of real excellence – that period between opening and subsequent discovery by the food columnists. On the plus side, the Parma Trat had not yet been written up. It also had its own liquor licence, meaning one did not have to trundle off to the nearest convenience store for a couple of bottles of awful wine in a brown paper bag. However, the trat did not come without drawbacks, notably a candle in a Chianti bottle thickly encrusted with multi-coloured wax, and a bright-eyed, bushy-tailed waiter who managed to screw up on just about everything but the rolls and butter. If you want good service avoid restaurants with red checked tablecloths.

No sooner had we seated ourselves and ordered Campari-soda, the drink you order when you don't want a drink, than Catherine leaned forward and said, "Geoffry, I was asleep at the switch when you called this morning. Why don't you and your niece both come for the weekend? There's plenty of room. And Robert, my son, will be out, so there'll be someone her own age. I presume she's been gently reared."

"Undoubtedly. My sister is nothing if not a good mother.

You must remember Mildred. She hasn't changed a bit; she's just more so. The trouble with Mildred is that she gives being good a bad name. She was born for challenge and crisis. She should have been an air raid warden during the London Blitz, or a missionary nun. Instead she married an academic and had three children. Her biggest challenge is chasing people with more than six items out of the express lane in the supermarket. She has pounded manners into the children."

"Good. Then you'll come?"

"You are a determined woman, Catherine. Yes, I'll, we'll come. Unless she has other plans."

"But you suggested on the phone she was at your disposal. Surely you weren't using her as an alibi to avoid a weekend in the country."

I looked up from my menu to see her tongue pushed firmly into her cheek. We both began to laugh.

It took a bit of gentle prodding to get Catherine to talk about herself. Those staunch good manners of a former era demanded she give me equal time. I could tell she had been the kind of hostess who said, "Tell me about yourself," to her first husband's friends, and braced herself to listen. It bores me to talk about myself; I know far too much about the subject already. I had no intention of redefining myself over the pasta, of creating a persona who spent Saturday afternoons at the museum, Sunday afternoons taking his old mother for a drive, and the rest of the week stealing time from his professional responsibilities to raise funds for worthy causes. It went without saying that this hypothetical persona would never drink too much, walk right past a crying child, or study the fit of the waiter's trousers. If the medium is indeed the message I preferred to keep my mouth shut.

The waiter took our order; it amused me to see he thought Catherine was my wife. More than just the right age, we were the same type, a resemblance heightened by our being the only English-speaking diners in the restaurant. Like a pair of gnus who have grazed their way into a herd of zebras, we mingled, but stood apart from the group.

As we ate our moderately good lunch and drank our over-priced wine, conversing in that inconsequential way people do when catching up on past time, I had an enormous sense of well-being. I remember being conscious of the feeling, principally, I suppose, because it happens so infrequently. But I was pleased to be seated across from this delightful woman over lunch, which I have always considered a more civilized meal than dinner.

"Considering how difficult you will be to please," she said over coffee, "is there anything you would like me to serve, or, more important, to avoid?"

"I am not a fussy feeder. I prefer fish heavily camouflaged. And I'm not really partial to beef. Beef, especially when rare, reminds me of the abattoir. For the rest I am easy. And I never eat desserts."

"You certainly don't have a weight problem," Catherine self-consciously batted her eyelashes. "Fine figure of a man, I'd say."

"You always did have taste. I don't eat desserts because I don't like sweet stuff."

"What a shame. I have a lovely recipe for a nuclear cloud layer cake. It's a torte, and it comes out looking just like the aftermath of a hydrogen explosion, particularly when it's smothered in whipped cream. I serve it with my atomic bombe: meringue filled with raspberry sherbet."

"Save them both for the volunteer committee luncheon."

I paid the cheque. The waiter stamped my Mastercard onto a Visa charge slip and had to correct his error. By now I had become resigned.

On the sidewalk outside the restaurant we stood, reluctant to say goodbye.

"Well, see you on Friday," she said. "I don't know whether to shake your hand or kiss your cheek."

"Why not do both?" I suggested, taking both her hands in mine. I kissed her after the continental fashion, on both cheeks. Then, from across the street, she turned, blew me a kiss, and blended into the flow of pedestrians walking east.

Back in my office that afternoon I was intermittently taken with the subversive idea that I might somehow postpone leaving for the country until Saturday morning. Some last minute, un-foreseen, totally fictitious event would require my presence in the city and delay my departure. That would get me out of Friday evening, and it is the evenings in the country that can seem endless. Days pass by without any real difficulty, but that stretch of time between the cocktail hour and bedtime, when one is held hostage to good manners, can limp by with agonizing slowness.

My desk tidy, I was on the point of leaving my office when the red light on my telephone flickered. I reached for the receiver.

"Geoffry Chadwick speaking."

"This is Madame Ludmilla, spiritualist, Tarot card reader, and all-around good time. If you cross my palm with gold I will tell you lies; if you don't I will tell you the truth. Bring your old martini glass and I will read the olives."

"Larry! Are you in Montreal?"

"You saw through my disguise. I am still in Toronto. How many faggots does it take to screw in a light bulb?"

"I have no idea." I hoped Gladys Walker did not happen to be listening.

"Two! And a pound of Crisco."

"As Santa Claus might say: Ho! Ho! Ho! What's on your mind?"

"Dinner with you this coming Friday. I'm coming through Montreal en route to visit friends, but I thought I might spend the evening in town, with my old chum. It's been so long. Do I have bad breath?"

"No, it's the dry scaly dandruff that drove us apart." Even as I was trading lines with Larry I was thinking fast. Did I really want to have dinner with Lawrence Townsend II, the Dr. Jekyll and Mr. Hyde of faggotdom. Sober, he can be bland to the point of invisibility, like the man who tries to sell you a photocopy machine in a TV commercial. But he drinks like a camel. Drunk, he becomes to homosexual men what the CN Tower is to a radio antenna. Dinner in Montreal with Larry always means a toot, for him anyway. Did I want an extended cocktail hour, followed by an alcoholic dinner, during which he would try to make the waiter, followed by a bit of bar hopping before he either picked someone up or went off to the baths? No, I didn't. It would mean driving out to the country with a hangover and starting the weekend squarely behind the eight ball.

"I can't," I lied glibly. "I'm off to the country myself."

"But you hate the country. I'm offering you a perfect excuse to slice one evening off the long weekend."

"Unfortunately my niece is involved. She'd be very disappointed not to leave on Friday. How about Monday?" Larry is always more domesticated after the weekend.

"Can't. I'll have to drive back to Toronto. Must be in the office Tuesday A.M. Ah, well, another broken dream."

"Larry, it is surmounting just such disappointments that builds character. And now I must dash, in a cloud of dust and small stones. I'll call you next time I get up to the big T-O, which ought to be in about three weeks."

I hung up, resigned to a Friday afternoon departure. Dinner in the country, dull though it might be, was a lesser evil than a riotous evening with Larry, the only man I know who offered to blow the cop who stopped him for going through a red light. Even though I have known him nearly all my life I still can't decide if he's a good friend or a bad habit.

It has been suggested that we are all bits of flotsam and jetsam thrown up by the river of life. Were that to be true then my mother is a tea bag. I waited impatiently in the carpeted lobby of Mother's apartment building while the uniformed security guard telephoned upstairs to say I wanted to go up. I had asked him why he even bothered getting the O.K. since he had seen me coming and going for some years now.

"Regulations, sir," he replied, lowering his voice as if imparting a confidence.

"How do you know this bunch of flowers is not really a submachine-gun wrapped in coloured paper?"

He laughed, a hollow, mechanical laugh. "I know you too well for that, sir."

"Then why can't I just go up?"

"Regulations, sir." This time he lowered his voice even further and wrinkled his forehead, as though his mimeographed sheets of procedures were really inscribed on parchment indentures.

I heard the housekeeper's voice come onto the line. I was announced, given clearance, and told to proceed. The laughable feature of Mother's apartment building is that the elderly residents do not need protection from the outside world, but from one another. Ovens remain on broil for days at a time, bathtubs overflow, mattresses smoulder. Most of the men are retired, most of the women widows. Bills go directly to their trust companies, including the ones for liquor, which is delivered by the case. They drink and play bridge; often they just drink.

Mother is right in her element. She no longer plays much bridge as she has to be reminded constantly what suit is trump. I suppose if I were asked how she spends her time I would have to say she drinks and smokes. Hardly a career, one might legitimately say, but when pursued with total concentration these activities while away the day.

Using my key I let myself into Mother's apartment.

"Geoffry, is that you?" called Mother from the living room.

"The very same. Life size and living colour," I said, attempting to be cheerful, as I crossed the handsome Bokara carpet to her wing chair and kissed her on the forehead. "A few spring flowers to cheer up a girl."

Mother took the bunch of flowers as though they were just one more problem with which she did not wish to deal.

"How's the hip?" I inquired.

"Better today. Be a dear, Geoffry, and ask Madame to put these in water."

"Shall I save a trip and top you up?"

"What a good idea."

I carried Mother's glass to the pantry along with the flowers. Monumental in her white uniform, Madame nodded a greeting. I asked her to arrange the flowers. Then I took an envelope out of my jacket pocket and put it onto the counter. "*Bonne chance.*" Inside were five mini-loto tickets. I admit I cultivate Madame. My head rests far easier on the pillow knowing she is in charge, checking to see Mother does not poison, drown, or incinerate herself.

I carried two vodkas back to the living room. "Has Elizabeth arrived?"

"She is having a bath. My goodness, how she has grown."

"In which direction? The last time I saw her she was tall enough to be my mother."

"Madame has made Irish stew. I always say you can't beat a good old Irish stew."

"To be old is good for antiques, Mother, but not for stew. Was it made within living memory?"

"Oh, Geoffry, you are turning into such an old woman. Madame made it this morning. Lamb, with lots of lovely fresh vegetables. Walter will be here any minute; I'll go and change."

Mother rose unsteadily to her feet and limped from the room, the limp due to a broken hip which took forever to calcify and had to be pinned. There is no calcium in vodka, and Mother won't touch milk, not even in tea. For Mother to say she was going to change was no more than a figure of speech. No matter which housecoat she puts on she always looks the same. Like most women of her age and income bracket Mother has a little dressmaker, with all that word implies: widowed, foreign, possessed of a cat and a sewing machine. To be a successful little dressmaker one must also live on a side street and cultivate an air of worried preoccupation, so that clients will feel demeaned to question the hefty bill submitted on notepaper. Mother's little dressmaker specializes in caftans, which I am sure she can sew in her sleep. Large, loose, flowing, they hang on Mother like collapsed parachutes.

The buzzer ran. "I'll get it," I called to Madame.

I opened the door to greet Walter Gordon, one of those really old family friends who can remember me in diapers. He still claims I only cried when I was picked up. In retrospect, I can see Walter had been a very positive influence when I was growing up. I embarked on childhood at a time when for a child to call any adult by his christian name was considered forward. The problem was skirted by tacking on "aunt" or "uncle" in front of the first name. Walter, however, refused to be adopted, explaining patiently to my mother, who in matters of social protocol was somewhere to the right of Queen Victoria, that since his name was indeed Walter, and since he and I were in no way related, why could I not use his first name. Mother tutted and clucked, but a door had been opened.

Although I did not realize it at the time, Walter had talked to me, not down to me. He asked my opinion, and listened, and replied. To be a bright child in a world of dense adults leaves a mark, not to say a scar. And Walter had his problems too, I came to realize. Being an unmarried man in those days carried a stigma. To be an unmarried woman meant you were not desirable enough to catch a man. To be an unmarried man in a world full of women dying to be asked meant one was, well, you know, a little light on his feet. But I can still remember Walter gave me my first real taste of being adult, and I was quickly hooked.

"Geoffry, I was hoping you'd be here." We shook hands.

"You are listening to a recorded announcement," I replied. "The Widow Chadwick is changing; the niece is in the tub; and I am on the sauce. The bar is open. Enter. Rest. Pray."

"Splendid." He beckoned to me conspiratorially. "Before the ladies join us you can help me with my novel."

One of the things I have always admired about Walter is that he takes being frivolous very seriously.

"So it's a novel today. Whatever happened to the musical comedy based on the life of St. Teresa, *Break the Habit?*"

"It's on hold. I am going to write a romance." The high-coloured face, a graph of wrinkles, took on a mock-serious expression. "*Rick Richardson, Male Nurse.* It's about a male nurse."

"No!"

"Yes. His name is Rick Richardson. And he's deeply, romantically in love with Floyd Lloyd, chief neurosurgeon. Hair greying at the temples and wonderfully sensitive hands with long tapering fingers. But there is also an orderly . . ."

"Who strides the hospital corridors with his coverall opened to the waist revealing hard golden pectorals."

"Exactly." By now we were in the living room whispering like third graders. "He's Polish, Januz, and speaks little English. But he has a searing slavic intensity."

"Do they trade eyelocks?"

"Eyelocks that leave poor Rick quite dizzy. In his head he loves Floyd Lloyd, but down there . . ."

"Walter, would you be offended if I pointed out that sacred and profane love, or brain versus brawn, has already been done?"

"But never with such a deft and stylish mixture of the romantic and the raunchy. However, I need a subplot, or at least a complication."

"How about . . . how about making him a single parent?" I suggested. "His wife ran off with her hairdresser, who then had a sex-change operation, and Rick gained custody of the wonderfully winsome, wise beyond his years, winning but bedwetting little lad. But only after a messy, no-holds-barred custody suit. To the victor goes the spoiled."

"But Rick doesn't want the boy to grow up gay like his father, so he goes to an encounter group for gay single fathers."

"It's called Date-a-Dad."

"No cheap shots, Geoffry. I am talking *Kunst*."

"Sorry. I guess I lost my head. Does he meet a frank, open, and toothsome daddy with a crewcut and laughing eyes, named Duane?"

"It just so happens that he does. So there is poor Rick, torn between Floyd, Januz, Duane."

"Who gets Rick in the end?"

"They all do. With Dr. Floyd it is transcendental, with Januz exhausting, with Duane wholesome. Rick and Duane decide to stay together for the children's sake. Weasel!"

"Walter, dearest." Mother made what she considered to be a gracious hostess entrance, somewhat hindered by her limp and having been on the vodka since noon. "How lovely you could come."

"How wonderful you're looking, Constance," lied Walter as he embraced Mother with some care so as not to upset her delicate balance. "It's been ages," he said, escorting her gallantly to her chair. "Now that you're up and about, practically on point, I'm delighted to see, we must have lunch."

"That would be lovely," replied Mother, who never left her apartment building unless it was absolutely imperative.

Walter understood this perfectly, but he continued to play
the game whose rules were truly written in tablets of stone: the
older one gets, the less one acknowledges the fact. At least such
was the case with people of my mother's generation. The second
childhood was less a time of incontinence and dribbling than a
tacit but absolute denial of the aging process. The word still
had power to people like my mother and Walter; to speak
something caused it to exist. Obversely, to remain silent meant
to deny, to refuse acknowledgement. I can still remember that
while my father lay dying of cancer not once did I ever hear the
word spoken by Mother or any of their mutual friends. Father
was ill; to admit he had cancer would have been equivalent to
passing sentence. It was the kind of thinking that defoliated
Vietnam.

"And thank you for the heavenly narcissus," continued
Mother pointing to a pot of pink hyacinth. They are as spring-
like as the first robin." She subsided into her wing chair in a
billow of cut black velvet; a rope of malachite beads clanked
across her washboard chest. "Ah, here she is."

We all turned to look at the door, where my niece Elizabeth
paused for a moment, framed. "Making the star's entrance?" I
asked. "I'm your lovable Uncle Geoffry, in case you don't remember. And this is Mr. Gordon. Walter, my niece Elizabeth Carson."

"How do you do, Mr. Gordon," said Elizabeth shaking hands.
"Hello, Uncle Geoffry." She spoke almost shyly.

"I think we might hazard a chaste embrace. I am your uncle,
after all." We held one another stiffly, for a second, as I gave her
a quick, antiseptic kiss on the lips. Can I get you something to
drink? A little white wine? Vermouth? Four fingers of neat
vodka?"

The girl smiled to reveal teeth which had no doubt sent her orthodontist on a Caribbean cruise. "White wine, please."

When my sister said on the telephone that Elizabeth had grown, what she meant was that the girl had turned into a young woman. The change was less an addition of height or weight than it was an alteration of contour. Areas of flatness had become curved; hollows had become planes; awkwardness, grace. She was beautiful with that clean, bland beauty of middle-class girls whose favourable genes have been reinfonced by well-balanced meals and vitamin supplements. The face, a perfect oval against long, straight, deep-brown hair, bore no traces of experience. I could not help thinking of Catherine, who must have looked much the same at eighteen.

"What do you think of my beautiful granddaughter?" asked Mother, a smile making her mouth even more crooked. Mother does not deliberately put on her lipstick over the lip line, like old movie sirens, she just aims the tube somewhere between her nose and her chin and hopes for the best.

"Charming, perfectly charming," replied Walter with beautifully honed insincerity. What else could he say?

"Elizabeth is going to be a singer," continued Mother as the girl seated herself on a needlepoint footstool beside her grandmother's chair. I handed her a glass of wine. "She's had ever so much experience: Gilbert and Sullivan and Franz Lehar, and she sang the role of Laurey in *Annie Get Your Gun*."

"Laurey is a character in *Oklahoma*," I corrected.

"No, *Carousel*." Mother had the bit between her teeth, as my father used to say. I knew the prospect of dinner guests always caused her to toss back a couple of extra vodkas. "And she is coming to Montreal to prepare for a big career. I hope she will sing opera. You will sing opera, won't you, dear? Have you been watching those Wagner operas on public broadcasting? *The Lord of the Rings?* Splendid, simply magnificent. I confess I did shed a tear when Wotan put his daughter Leonora to sleep, but the gnomes! They were all wearing hard hats, just like construction workers. They made me think of those mechanical dolls who are forever building things down in Fraggle Rock."

She wheezed with laughter. I was beginning to get a little apprehensive. When Mother becomes really animated it is generally a prelude to disaster.

"That's a lovely shade of blue, dear." Mother approvingly patted the shoulder of my niece's teal-blue granny dress. You know, I have a lovely string of chalcedony beads which I never wear. They would be lovely with your frock. I'll just go and fetch them.

Mother levered herself to her feet and pointed herself at the door.

At the merest mention of opera Walter perked right up. One of the litmus tests of your twenty-four-carat queen is whether or not he likes opera. Something as profoundly silly as opera that takes itself so seriously naturally appeals to the camp sensibility. Walter can reminisce by the hour on past performances: Flagstad as Seglinde, Callas as Norma, Pinza as Don Giovanni.

"What will you be singing for your audition?" he asked Elizabeth.

"Two songs from *Frauenliebe und Leben*; some Fauré: 'Claire de Lune' and 'Mandoline.' For my aria I will sing 'Caro Nome' from *Rigoletto*."

"The most beautiful Gilda I ever heard . . ." began Walter.

I caught sight of Madame giving me a sign from the front

hall. "Excuse me," I said, leaving the room.

"*Monsieur Geoffry, Madame Chadwick est endormie.*"

When Madame says, "Mrs. Chadwick is asleep," it means Mother has passed out cold. I told Madame to put her to bed and to keep a serving of dinner warm in case she was hungry when she woke up.

"A slight change of plans," I said a shade brightly when I returned to the living room. "Your grandmother is feeling a bit unwell, so she has gone to lie down." I did not dare look at Walter; we have both played this scene many times before.

I took them both out to dinner at a Chinese restaurant, for which Elizabeth had expressed a preference. Chinese food is really dreary: much ado about little protein. And all that monosodium glutamate has me doing the dehydration waltz at three A.M. But I did not have to say much. Walter went on at length about opera and singers he had heard in recital. Who can resist the pull of a captive audience? I played games with my food, using my ineptitude with chopsticks as an excuse not to eat.

After leaving Walter at his apartment building, I drove Elizabeth back to Mother's and told her about the invitation we had both received for the weekend. She replied it sounded super, an all-purpose WASP word used to describe anything not downright repulsive. I then took a detour and picked up a double cheeseburger to go which I ate in my bathrobe over the kitchen sink. There is much to be said for the corrupt West.

III

The rest of the week passed, as it has a way of doing, one tiny second following another. After working two days in an office where hushed tones and three-piece suits, greyed pastels and Homburgs on the hat rack were the rule, Gladys Walker managed to get a partial message. She began to cover herself up to the neck and left the Nefertiti pendant at home. The ankle bracelet remained, and she still wore high heels that must have murdered her metatarsals. She also continued to cantilever her bust. I expect secretaries to wear clothes from Ogilvy's, not Frederick's of Hollywood.

Friday arrived and with it the immediate prospect of departure for the country. As promised, Catherine had sent me a map. On holiday weekends Montrealers swarm off the island like lemmings, and the main problem is avoiding peak traffic on the bridges. I telephoned my niece and said I would collect her at half-past three. I urged her to be ready.

To my pleasant surprise Elizabeth was waiting downstairs in the lobby of Mother's building. I put her suitcase into the trunk of my Cadillac, a car bought not for show but for safety.

The most expedient way for us to leave the island was via the Champlain Bridge. Just about three years ago on this same bridge I was involved in a bad accident. My own car, which had been stolen by a punk, crashed and rolled over. I jumped from the taxi in which I had been following and pulled him free from the

burning vehicle, which then exploded. The blast threw me to
the ground and cracked three ribs. The man I rescued had died
in the crash. It was a messy accident, and I have not been able
since to drive across the Champlain Bridge without my scalp
going prickly.

On this particular afternoon, however, we moved smoothly
across, the traffic heavy but not yet congested. In short order
we were on the Eastern Townships Autoroute on our way to the
great adventure.

I eased into the cruising lane of the divided highway heading
southeast. It took me some seconds to shake a station-wagon,
bursting with people, which was tailgating my car. I try to stay
away from any vehicle carrying three generations of passengers.
Once clear, I relaxed enough to ask my niece how her audition
had gone. She replied that she had been quite nervous at first,
and the accompanist played at an uncomfortably slow tempo;
however she had gained confidence as she went along and sang
her aria quite well. The teacher had agreed to take her on in
the fall.

"Aside from a love of singing," I began, "do you really want
to be a performer? It's one thing to have a pretty voice and like
music; it's something else to face an auditorium full of people
and try to tell them something new about the music."

"I realize that, Uncle Geoffry, and I don't yet know the answer.
I guess I'll have to find out as I study."

Her answer seemed reasonable. "What does your mother think
about your making a career in music? Wouldn't she prefer you
to be a nurse or a librarian, something conservative with coffee
breaks and a pension plan?"

"I guess so. But Richard's being at Juilliard made things easier for me. I think by this time Mother is resigned."

My nephew, the eldest of Mildred's three children, was a harpsichord major at Juilliard. I wasn't sure about his talent; but I did know he was handsome, homosexual, and humourless. I suspected he would go far.

"Jennifer wants to be an elementary school teacher," my niece continued, "and being the youngest she walks on water."

I laughed out loud. The observation struck me as odd, considering its source. Had I underestimated this girl, dismissing her because she was not an extrovert?

"I can understand her wanting to be a teacher," I said. "It's a good, respectable, dull profession. But why would she want to teach elementary school? She will never meet any grownups, certainly not among faculty members. Her mind will turn to mush."

"She says the early formative influences are the strongest, and that kindergarten is the place to develop the correct attitudes towards learning."

"But getting back to you, Elizabeth. Supposing you do decide to become a performer. It takes a great many skills besides mere talent. Just look at the number of aspiring young musicians playing for loose change in the subway. Are you a good sight-reader? As that laid-back Muppet musician in the uniform might say, 'Can you follow the dots?' "

She gave a little self-conscious laugh. "Fairly well."

"Are you working at an instrument as well as voice?"

"I've been studying piano for eight years."

"Good. Are you studying languages, especially French and German?"

"I studied French at school."

"You'd better get cracking on German," I suggested. "It seems to me that now is the time you should be reading through the principal song cycles: *Die Schöne Mullerin, Les Nuits d'Eté, Liederkreis*, getting to know them, coming to grips with the problems, growing up to them, as it were, just the way an actor grows into a role like Hamlet or Lear."

"How come you know so much about the song repertoire, Uncle Geoffry? I thought you were supposed to be a lawyer."

I suppose at eighteen everyone has a right to be fatuous. How dare you know anything outside of your own narrow specialty? I smiled and shrugged; I did not feel it necessary to reply.

Chris and I used to listen to music a lot, not grimly, as though to speak while a record played were sacrilege, but easily, the music a pleasant background for a drink, or dinner at my apartment. I have a small but fairly eclectic collection of records, something for almost every taste. I appeared to have surprised my niece, but I too at one point knew very little about the art song repertoire. That was before I managed to get mixed up with someone who owned six recordings of *Frauenliebe und Leben* . . . .

I had met Peter Piper at a party one April evening, the kind of party one attends in the hopes of finding Prince Charming, at least for the weekend. There were no ladies present, although I speak purely biologically. The host owned an immensely powerful hi-fi along with recordings of just about every musical comedy ever produced on Broadway. When I arrived Ethel Merman was announcing to the world at large that she was going to get off her butt and out of the living room and onto the Orpheum circuit. Miss Merman made the announcement in the voice of Stentor with the volume control at a quarter to twelve.

I fled at once to the kitchen and dived into a highball. The din coming from the front room flowed down the hallway like water, tangible, tactile, tightroping along the threshold of pain. A man came into the kitchen, around my age, I guess. He had that corduroy, suede, horn-rimmed, slightly rumpled look that always makes me feel, well, shall we say maternal.

"Loud, isn't it?" I said.

He smiled, a winsome, little-boy-lost smile. I began to wonder if the evening was going to be so dreary after all.

"Just a bit," he replied.

"I'm Geoffry Chadwick," I said, extending my hand.

"Peter Piper." We shook hands.

"Good manners dictate I plunge in there and mix. Self-preservation suggests I remain here."

Peter Piper smiled. "You're the first man I've met tonight who didn't say it."

"Say what?"

"Say, on being introduced, 'Peter Piper picked a peck of pickled peckers.'"

"One of the most blatant heterosexual myths is that gay conversation is bright, brittle, bitchy, and oh-so-clever. The last time I was here one of the guests kept declaiming: 'They're changing guards at Buckingham Palace. Christopher Robin went down on Alice.' Then he became so convulsed with laughter he couldn't go on. Ringing changes on your name is of that same high level of sophistication. Although I do think Mr. and Mrs. Piper Senior might have saved you a lot of flak had they named you David or John or Bruce."

"I was named after a grandfather. Do you like Strauss?"

The non sequitur caught me off guard. "You mean as in 'May I have this waltz?'"

"No, not Johann, Richard."

"I suppose so. I can't say I know his music that well. *Der Rosenkavalier*; *Till Eulenspiegel's Merry Pranks*. I once went to a performance of *Salomé*. I remember thinking that John the Baptist, patron saint of the Province of Quebec, lost his head over a topless dancer. For the rest I found it turgid. Why?"

"I just bought a new recording of the *Four Last Songs*."

"Are you suggesting, I hope, that we sneak out of here by the rear door, go back to your place, and play it?"

"Something like that."

As I drove I tried to keep my eyes on the road and off the auburn hair tumbling over the clean profile, but the windshield was beginning to steam up with crotch fog.

The apartment echoed the man; warm, chaotic, but with an underlying organizing principle which centred on the most elaborate mechanism for playing records I had yet seen. Ceiling to floor, walls held cabinets for records, hundreds at a quick estimate, yet filed and labelled with absolute precision. We listened to the *Four Last Songs*, and to *Die Schöne Mullerin* as well. Thank goodness he had scotch.

After the young man in the songs had drowned himself in the babbling brook on account of the miller's beautiful but fickle daughter, we finally got down to business. It was delightful. Peter turned out to be passionate and loving, in that absent-minded way, almost as if sex had taken him by surprise. I admired his body as he sprang from the post-coital couch to play a recording of *Frauenliebe und Leben*, a tactless choice under the circumstances.

Peter and I began what I suppose could be called an affiar. I, on the other hand, began what turned out to be a total immersion crash course in the art song, more precisely the German art song. We made occasional side trips into the French. We wandered in the woods with Berlioz, picking lilies of the valley and wild strawberries. With Debussy and Fauré we watched pale ladies and pallid suitors drift through moonlit gardens to the sound of mandolins and plangent fountains. But mostly we remained firmly within the land of the *lied*.

When I first met Peter it was spring, and although we were too worldly to speak of love, we "saw" each other almost every evening. Spring: *Fruhling*. Were it not for spring there would be no German art song, no *lied*. Schubert, Schumann, Strauss, whose very names sound like someone spraying rose bushes, all wrote of spring. And I listened to them all. *Die Winterreise, Vier Ernste Gesange, Lieder Eines Faharenden Gesellen*; the names sound like an automobile stuck in snow. And I listened to them as well, mutely following the word sheets as Peter did not permit talking when music played. I would have traded my soul for a little Italian opera, a few *addios, piètas, t'amos*, but Italy remained a foreign land, a distant shore visited only by those who did not know better.

Peter worked for an insurance company. I learned little else about him other than that he was obsessed with the art of singing. He did not sing himself; he did not play an instrument; he read music only on the level of Dick and Jane. He remained the Compleat Listener. And even though my skin loved his skin, I knew we were only marking time.

It turned out to be one of his "comparison" evenings that drove us apart. Occasionally, on a whim, a whim of iron, he would get hooked on a particular song and play seven different recordings, one after another. It was enough to make the strongest man break down and confess. On this particular evening number one on the hit parade was *"Fruhling"* from the *Four Last Songs.*

"They're playing our song," I remarked after the third hearing.

"Shhh. Listen to how she sings: *"Nun liegst du erschlossen/ in Gleiss und Zier.'* 'Now you stand revealed in glitter and glory.' "

"How can she even keep her face straight for a line like that? And now, my dear Peter, I would like a drink, and some Cole Porter. Better still, silence. Then we are going to bed. And I do not want *Songs on the Death of Children* as mood music." I reached out and pressed the eject button, cutting off the soprano in mid-phrase.

"If you are bored, Geoffry, no one is forcing you to stay."

"*Auf wiedersehen.* I'll leave you to play "Spring" thirteen more times. As the actress said to the bishop, baby: 'There may be autumn in my hair but there's still spring in my ass.' " As I opened the door to his apartment I turned to wave one last ironic goodbye, but he was bent over the turntable changing the record.

Some months later I ran into him. He was just coming out of a record store with a package under his arm which looked like a medium-sized pizza.

"Why, Geoffry, how are you? Haven't seen you in a while." He smiled, little-boy-lost. My skin began to tingle. "Why not come back for a drink?"

I looked at his beautiful nose and clear, candid eyes, at the soft auburn hair falling across the broad, untroubled forehead, and my impulse was to say yes. Then I looked at the package under his arm and remembered the *Kindertotenlieder.*

"I'm sorry, Peter," I said. "I have an engagement. Why don't I give you a call?"

He nodded and walked away . . . .

"Uncle Geoffry?"

"Oh, sorry, Elizabeth. I must have been woolgathering. Is our turnoff coming up soon?"

Elizabeth consulted the map. "It should be the next exit, then straight ahead on the secondary road for about thirteen miles."

IV

Catherine's map turned out to be accurate. About fifteen minutes later we turned into the long gravel driveway leading down to a large white house and pulled to a stop at the front door. I confess that for just a second I toyed with the idea of throwing the engine into reverse and heading backwards up the driveway I had just driven down.

"Here we are," I announced flatly as I pressed the switch which released the locks on both doors. I opened my own door and got out. At once I was sorry I had done so.

From around the corner of the house poured two enormous English sheepdogs, excitedly barking greetings. Far from making me feel like an intruder, they overwhelmed me with unwelcome welcome. I was butted repeatedly in the crotch, goosed three times by a large wet nose, and nearly knocked off my feet. Fortunately Elizabeth came to my rescue, clapping her hands to get the beasts' attention and bending down to have her face soundly licked.

"Grendel! Caliban! Sit!" At the sound of their master's voice both dogs sat, their backsides squirming with pleasure as Catherine came through the front door to greet us.

"Geoffry," she kissed me lightly on the cheek. "And this must be your niece."

"Elizabeth Carson, Mrs. Bradford," I said by way of

introduction.

"Catherine Bradford," she said, shaking hands with Elizabeth. "I see you've already met the dogs."

"I'll say. And very Jean Harlow they are too," I quipped.

"Jean who?"

"Harlow, Catherine dear. She was a movie star, in case you don't remember. She made a movie called *Bombshell* in which she appeared with two of those sheepdogs. Her leading man was Franchot Tone. He was once married to Joan Crawford."

"Joan who?" Catherine gave me a wink. "Wasn't she before my time? Geoffry dearest, I grew up on Gidget. Now let me show you to your rooms."

By appearances, Catherine's house had been built at a time when a summer house was considered just that, a second residence to be opened up in May and shut down in October. The building rambled, its rooms high and spacious, the corridors and stairwell generously proportioned. Only recently had the house been made habitable for winter, I heard Catherine explaining to Elizabeth as she led her up the stairs. Insulation had been blown into the attic, aluminum siding attached to the outside walls, double windows installed.

While Elizabeth was being shown to her room I put down my suitcase and wandered into the living room to find out what I had really let myself in for. The room could loosely be described as eclectic. Dominating one wall a fieldstone fireplace and chimney rose to the ceiling whose rough, unfinished beams had a slight sheen, as though coated with varethane. From either end of a mantelpiece, hewed no doubt from a single block of birch, two antique copper kettles pointed their spouts at one another like accusing fingers. At the far end of the room a

sectional couch, upholstered in something rough-textured and
practical, sat under a window overlooking the lake. Directly
opposite, to the right of the door leading to the hall, a bow window, fitted with small panes of glass, looked onto the driveway.
A window-seat, inviting to the eye, hostile to back and back-
side, filled the bow. Two armchairs flanked the fireplace; two
more faced it from across the room. All were upholstered in
chintz, the last resort of the do-it-yourself decorator, in muted
tones of sage green and ochre.

The most unusual furnishing in the room was a pair of low
tables, in front of the couch and window-seat respectively. On
top of two logs, planed flat on top and bottom, rested thick slabs
of maple waxed or varathaned to a high gloss. The logs themselves had been sanded to satin, and like the beams in the ceiling
they glittered with Varathane. The effect was of suburban rusti-
city, of natural materials tidied up and tamed, of the wilderness
led quietly indoors. It went hand in hand with hiking along
carefully marked trails in designer boots, sleeping in nylon
tents, paddling aluminum canoes. Even the kettles, cast to sit
on the back of a wood stove, looked a little forlorn, like the
brass coal scuttle filled with magazines, reduced as they all were
from useful objects to decorating accents. The coal scuttle sat
on one side of a fire screen with brass handles and beside a
wrought-iron stand from which hung regulation fireplace
utensils. Predictably the andirons were a pair of cast iron owls,
complete with yellow glass eyes. Show me a country house that
doesn't have an owl motif somewhere and I'll show you a tent.

To my taste anyway, the most interesting object in the room
was the rubbing of a medieval knight hanging on the wall facing
the fireplace. Putting on my Benjamin Franklin half-spectacles,

I read the small brass plate secured to the plain wooden frame. "Sir William Fitzralph, Essex, 1323." He cut a dashing figure, did Sir William, his armour combining the best features of both chain-mail and plate armour. From his left shoulder hung a shield, from his waist a long sword in a beautifully wrought scabbard; at his feet crouched a mastiff, symbol of loyalty. His hands in their chain-mail mittens were pressed together in an attitude of piety, while his eyes gazed steadfastly at the viewer. I thought him splendid, Sir William son of Ralph; and with his attitude of pious militancy he was as contemporary as a computer.

Hearing Catherine coming downstairs I went back into the front hall.

She explained to me that off the hallway leading to the kitchen lurked two small bedrooms, once occupied by maids, and separated by a bathroom. The rooms were small but comfortably appointed. "There is a larger guest room upstairs," she said, "but you would be right in the middle of everything and everyone. In addition to all of us, Father asked if he could come out for the weekend. I was certain you would prefer to be downstairs where you can be more private."

"Correct."

"You can have either of the two rooms, but there's a small problem about the bathroom I had promised you would have to yourself. I hadn't known at the time that my husband Mark had invited one of his former real estate colleagues up from Toronto for the weekend. Do you mind awfully sharing the bathroom with one other person?" She smiled reassuringly. "I promise to nip in hourly with a can of scouring powder and a damp rag. Now don't look glum, Geoffry. You're here to have a good time."

"Tell me about it."

"And now I have to drive into town for some last-minute errands. That's the trouble with life in the country. You have to drive five miles for a loaf of bread. Elizabeth said she would like to come along with me. Mark's playing golf with my father. He may be back before me, but he doesn't bite. Please don't bite him. Now I'll leave you. The liquor is in the dining room and the love letters are in the top drawer of the night-table in the master bedroom. Keep yourself amused."

She smiled and left. I had to admit Catherine was one of the few women I know who looks good in pants.

I unpacked my admittedly meagre supply of casual clothing. A madras shirt with a button-down collar and a pair of L.L. Bean chinos are about as adventurous as I ever get. I changed, shedding the three-piece suit, then carried my forty ounces of Black Label and half-gallon of vodka to leave on the bar. Not for me that amusing little hostess gift, six Aynsley egg coddlers or a machine for making your own pasta. Liquor is a dull, safe present. And I am the first to admit the element of self-interest involved. To be marooned in the country with the liquor running out must be roughly equivalent to Dante's sixth circle of hell.

A door to the left of the fireplace led from the living room onto a wide covered porch which overlooked the lake. It commanded what any real estate agent would have called a superb view, although fresh water looks to me like consommé. On the far side of the lake stood houses to which distance lent charm, as it did to tinkertoy automobiles travelling a narrow stripe of road. Beyond further fields, squares on a quilt, a large untidy mountain sprawled across the landscape like a beached blue whale, effectively blocking out whatever lay on the other side.

A dull roar approaching from stage right became visible as a large white launch, powered by an outboard motor. It snarled past my line of vision, the owner obviously uncaring about the price of gas, the passengers numb with noise. This aggressive racket, a violation of the rural tranquility, struck me as far more offensive than the occasional accent of sound which disturbs the low and steady hum of the city.

A short flight of steps led from the porch down to a patio which, I was relieved to see, was paved with flagstones, not railway ties. From just beyond the low cedar hedge surrounding the patio, the contour of the land fell away sharply to the shoreline. Secure in my rubber-soled Wallabies I set off to investigate the property. What started out to be a solitary ramble shortly took on the dimensions of a royal progression as the dogs, dying for diversion, took off after me in enthusiastic pursuit. As they went crashing through the underbrush I could not help thinking that those long woolly coats must provide a halfway house for every flea, tick, and burr in the neighbourhood.

An opening had been cut through a thicket of small cedar trees. I followed the path down to the shore where it opened onto a wide strip of pebbly beach. To the right of the beach a concrete pier jutted about twenty-five feet into the water. I could see where the effect of the prevailing wind had caused the waves to wash sand into the shallow area protected by the jetty. It must be a good place to swim, for those who like to swim. I do not much care for swimming, least of all in freshwater lakes whose muddy bottoms nurture slimy plants waiting to wrap their stems around the legs of those indolent enough to tread water.

One of the dogs, I knew I would never learn to tell them apart, galloped up to me with a well-chewed stick in his mouth, obviously a favourite toy. Dropping the unsavoury object at my feet, he began to dash back and forth between me and the water, barking excitedly. Taking my cue – we are all, after all, God's creatures – I threw the stick as far as I could into the lake. Without a second's hesitation the beast plunged into the bitterly cold water, which a scant two months ago had probably been covered in ice. Grabbing the stick in his mouth he swam strongly back to shore, ran up to me, and dropped the stick obligingly at my feet.

Then he shook himself vigorously. A cloud of icy cold drops covered me from face to foot as I stood, motionless, trying to pretend I was somewhere else.

From behind me a voice, as familiar as my own, spoke my name. "Geoffry Chadwick."

Startled almost speechless, I turned. "Mark, Mark Crosby."

A feeling of intense discomfort rendered us temporarily mute before we fell back on protocol and shook hands.

"Unless this is some kind of terrible impractical joke, you must be married to Catherine."

"Yes. You appear surprised. Didn't she mention my name?"

"Not really. She spoke of her husband Mark. And since I knew she had gone back to her maiden name, your surname never came up."

"I must admit I was forewarned. Catherine said she had invited an old friend for the weekend, Geoffry Chadwick, who was once married to her cousin. I had time to get used to the idea, but I find myself quite disarmed at seeing you again."

We lapsed into that embarrassed silence of two people who really do not know what to say next. In everyone's life there is always someone who got away. In my own life it was Mark

Crosby. Now as he stood beside me, I felt haunted by the ghost of a remembered emotion.

"You're looking good, Mark. But why not? You have a beautiful and charming wife. And this isn't a bad pad." I made a gesture which encompassed house and grounds.

"I could say the same for you, Geoff – Geoffry. Grey hair suits you. You would look perfect in one of those 'Men of distinction drink' advertisements."

"Speaking of drinks, I could use one at this very second."

Mark led the way back up the path just a shade too quickly for my comfort. Country living, fresh air, and exercise obviously suited him. Although we were close to the same age I was forced to admit he looked considerably younger than I. After all these years he had kept his figure, still tall and elegant. His short brown hair was only sprinkled with grey.

When we walked into the living room, Mr. Bradford was seated there.

"How are you, sir? It's certainly been a while."

He stood up to shake hands. Mr. Bradford had always been punctilious about protocol. "It certainly has, Geoffry. How's your mother?"

One of these days I will meet someone over sixty-five who will inquire after my health instead of my mother's, and I won't know what to answer.

"Quite well, thank you, sir. She had a bad fall last year and broke her hip. But she's walking quite well these days."

"I'm glad to hear it. Haven't seen her for years. I myself keep fit as a fiddle playing golf. In the winter I go to Georgia. I must admit I drive a golf cart these days. Silver threads among the gold, and all that sort of thing. But I hope to be driving around in my golf cart until the day I die, with my boots on."

"Isn't that putting the cart before the hearse?"

He laughed, a hearty, hollow, mirthless laugh, and sat down again. I remembered him as a much younger man being a nit-picker, and age does not really change a person. It only makes him more so. Mr. Bradford opened car doors for ladies, held chairs, sprang to his feet when they entered the room. He cultivated clichés. His mind was a hothouse where wilted turns of phrase dug roots into potting soil and blossomed anew. A rolling stone gathered no moss in Mr. Bradford's mental land-scape. The early bird caught a protein-rich worm. This same bird in the hand was worth two of its friends in the bush, except, of course, when it was flocking together with others of its ilk. I could not be certain, but I'd almost be willing to bet that somewhere in his house he had a shoe box filled with neatly coiled and knotted bits of string. After all, you never knew. I'd also be willing to wager he always wet his finger before turning a page.

I bowed slightly and followed Mark to the dining room, where he poured two belts of scotch.

"You're joining me," I observed. "Good. It makes me feel less spineless and self-indulgent. Well, here's to . . ."

"Here's to . . ." he echoed, equally at a loss.

"Here's to surviving the weekend." As we drank, Mark looked straight into my eyes, and I realized that although some things may stop they do not necessarily go away.

It's going to be a full house this weekend," he continued. "Did Catherine warn you? Her son Robert is coming out, and I've invited a friend I used to work with when I sold real estate in Toronto."

"I understand we're to share a bathroom. Is he housebroken?"

"I think you'll enjoy Larry." Mark lowered his voice, about to impart a confidence. "He's as queer as a three-dollar bill." He gave a self-conscious wink. Then, as if to soften the blow of his comment, "But funny as hell."

"Wait a minute. You are not referring by any remote chance to a homophile real estate dealer yclept Lawrence Townsend II?"

"The very same. Do you know him?"

"Does Eaton's know Simpsons? Now if you'll excuse me, I'll just go and pack. If I have one more surprise today I shall retire to the Montreal General for a week."

Mark laughed. "You really haven't changed. You haven't even mellowed. Don't worry about Larry. He's very adept at concealing his true colours."

We moved back to the now empty living room. From the bow window we watched an Oldsmobile coming down the driveway.

"Let me get this one," I said, heading for the door. "Attack is the best means of defence."

I strode across the gravel in time to open the Oldsmobile door on the driver's side. "Welcome to the Townships, Lawrence T-II."

If Larry was surprised he did not let it show. "Give me a synonym for woman ending in u-n-t."

"Can't guess."

"Aunt! You dirty old thing." He swung himself out of the car. "Do we shake hands? Or shall I kneel and kiss the ring?"

"We are sharing a bathroom, in the west wing. Now we will govern ourselves accordingly, that is if we want to live to collect the old-age pension."

"Stay as sweet as you are. And think of the fun we'll have,

sitting up late in our jammies, sharing secrets and drinking scotch through a straw. Believe it or not, Faeceface, I'm glad to see you. Now how about one tiny smile for the camera. Cheese?"

"Feta!" I hissed, leaning on the F.

An electric-blue Corvette pulled into the driveway and came to a stop behind Larry's car. A young man, obviously Catherine's son, got out and smiled at Larry and me.

"You must be Robert," I said. "I'm Geoffry Chadwick and this is Lawrence Townsend."

"How do you do, sir, Mr. Townsend." He shook hands with both of us. The sun struck light from the bit of blue glass in his school ring.

The young man was undeniably handsome, if you happen to like the type. I have never had much of a sweet-tooth for that high-school, football hero clone. By thirty they are running to fat.

As he reached into his car to pick up his overnight bag, Larry sidled up to me. "I've just fallen in love," he whispered. "Do you suppose he might be willing to be my man Friday, to Monday?"

I placed a restraining hand on Larry's arm as the young man headed towards the house. "Watch me, Larry. Read my lips. Do not mess around. He may not be a minor, but he is not for you."

"I corrupted a miner once. He worked in Thetford Mines, but I met him on a three-day drunk in Quebec City. Spoke no English, and I spoke no French."

"But you spoke the language of love, right?"

"You might say."

I crossed the driveway to the front door. "If you will excuse me for a few minutes," I said to Mark who had come to stand on the front step. "I'm going to take a nap. The drink and all. It's been a busy week. I'm sure you understand."

V

I wasn't the least bit sleepy. In fact, seldom had I been more wide awake. But I had to get away for a while, to sort out the unfamiliar situation in which I found myself. I was in the country; my host turned out to have been my lover; my bathroommate had to be the biggest roundheel to ever come down the pike. Far from a bucolic idyll, the weekend was rapidly turning into the Plouffes visit Dallas.

I shut the door of my small bedroom and lay down. For want of something better, I reached for the novel I had tossed into my suitcase, a novel which Mother had simply adored, insisting I read it at once. It turned out to be one of those books nobody but the British can write, in which animals not only talk but do so in rolling Jacobean cadences. Even if animals were able to talk I doubt they would have anything to say I really wanted to hear.

I tossed the novel aside and picked up a legal journal, one of several I had also brought along. Not even an article on corporate takeovers could grab me, so I closed my eyes and tried to convince myself I wanted to sleep . . . .

When it comes to hindsight I have 20-20 vision. Those times in a life when one falls in love and believes it will last forever are generally when one is young, inexperienced, and too emotionally inept to sustain intimacy. By the time one has reached an age where it is possible to live closely with another person, one has come to realize it is impossible to achieve a state of transcendence through that other person. Although I am not a religious man, I have observed that in all major religions, salvation, for want of a better word, is a solitary act. But when one is young, one looks to others to help escape the narrow confines of self. Today young people use drugs, but I go back to an earlier, possibly less sophisticated time.

I had met Mark Crosby during a particularly unsettled period of my life, just after Susan and our baby daughter had been killed in the automobile accident. Once my initial grief had subsided, as with the passage of time it must, I found myself metamorphosed into a mysterious and glamorous figure in the eyes of my immediate world, that of young widower. For someone who has always fancied Restoration comedy, to find myself cast as the Byronic hero was a bit of a burden. I moved in a world of hushed voices, lugubrious looks, unguent understanding, compassion the consistency of caramel. Needless to say the erotic overtones were almost deafening.

As if being the Bereaved of the Year weren't enough, I was also coming to terms with the fact that I was homosexual. I certainly was not gay. Morose, moody, at times manic, I remained a far remove from that most misappropriated of words.

Although homosexual men often meet in bizarre, off-beat, and socially unacceptable places, the unbelieveably corny thing about Mark and me is that we met at a party, moreover a party of unimpeachable heterosexuality. The other guests were mostly people from the set in which my wife and I used to move. I had the distinct impression I was being kept track of. Once a decent period of mourning had elapsed I would be back in the marriage market. Unlike a divorced man, a widower, particularly a young one, has not had time to grow disillusioned with the institution of matrimony.

I remembered that particular party for a number of reasons. The hostess, who obviously harboured designs on my innocent flesh, had just discovered Bitter Lemon, a singularly unpalatable mix. It was a vodka party. Her Salvation Army apartment had been turned into a dascha. We said things like "*Nazdrovia*" and "What is to be done?" as we hoisted our vodka and sour lemon, vodka and quinine water, or vodka and tap water.

Mark Crosby came as the new kid on the block, as it were. He was a new face and definitely up for grabs. I remember shaking his hand and saying, "How do you do." That was all I said. But we spent the entire evening trading looks, that kind of eye contact which is half glance, half nelson. At one point we found ourselves side by side at the bar.

"I am leaving soon," I said. "Will you join me for a drink of scotch in, say, half an hour?"

He nodded. I just happened to have, tucked into the breast pocket of my jacket, my business card with my home address and phone number written on the back. With a quick gesture I transferred it from my jacket pocket to his.

Next I applied myself to the task of prying myself loose from the party. I have yet to meet a hostess who will relinquish a male guest without a struggle. "It's early. Have another drink. Tomorrow is Saturday after all," and the rest of those facist demands that masquerade as hospitality.

Guile reinforced by acute hot-pants gave me strength, and I managed to get away. Twenty-five minutes later Mark rang my bell. We didn't waste time talking. We didn't even pause for that proffered drink. We just undressed and went to bed and took turns fucking each other's brains out until the following afternoon . . . .

A knock sounded at my bedroom door, bringing me back to the present. "Come in," I said.

The door opened to reveal Larry dressed in stiff new jeans and a red checked lumberjack shirt. "Schlepping beauty, it's your fairy prince, come to wake you with a kiss."

"I'd sooner be given a hickey by Dracula."

"On your feet, Chadwick. What's with this nap shit? You're no more sleepy than I am. You're not going to spend the entire weekend barricaded in your room, are you? I've already lost out on the son. He's met your niece and they're well on their way to making their own Swedish movie. By midnight you won't be able to pry them apart with a crowbar. Is she on the Pill? She's sure as hell going to be under him."

"Christ, I hope so. Mildred will have my head if her daughter arrives back in Toronto pregnant. Where are they?"

"Taking a walk in the woods. Ho! Ho! Ho! If she shows up with pine needles stuck to the back of her skirt you're in big trouble."

"With friends like you who needs enemies?" I swung my feet onto the floor. "Larry, I can't figure out what you are doing here. The quiet country weekend is not really your scene."

"You're right. It's not. But I always liked working with Mark, even if he is clenched. He's a good salesman. Not my type though. Far too piss-elegant. And Catherine is one of the few women I know who is not a broad. Let's have a drink."

Going into the bathroom to wash my face and hands I made the discovery that every available surface, the window-sill, the top of the toilet tank, the glass shelf above the handbasin, had been preempted by Larry's toilet articles.

"Sorry," he called through the shut door. "I didn't leave you very much room."

"No, you didn't. You've got enough deodorant here for the Statue of Liberty. And kindly take your douche bag out of the toothbrush glass."

"It isn't in the toothbrush glass, Geoffry my sweet. You just said that to be disagreeable. Now hurry up. I can't face this weekend alone."

I emerged. "Do you suppose we are expected to change for dinner?"

"I hope not. Don't I look just too divinely butch? I was going to wear my Kodiak fuck-me boots, but they're so goddamn hot they make my corns pop."

"To the bar!" I commanded. "Forward!"

After I made myself a drink, I wandered back down the short hallway to the kitchen where Catherine had tied herself into an apron and appeared to be doing something at the stove. I asked if there was anything I could do. Like most offers of help it was genuinely insincere; consequently I was not a little taken aback when she suggested I prepare the beans. In short order I found myself seated at the kitchen table facing a knife, a colander, and a mound of raw green beans.

"Catherine," I began, "I'm surprised that in an establishment this size which is full of people you don't have a housekeeper, or *une bonne à tout faire*."

"I do, but she is terribly accident prone. She puts out eggs for the soufflé and they throw themselves onto the floor. She is presently at home with five stitches in her hand because the can of tuna she was opening turned on her. So this weekend I am grateful for any help I can get."

As a matter of fact, to sit quietly in the kitchen, my hands occupied, talking with Catherine, was pleasanter than I could have imagined. To live alone begins as a choice and ends up as a habit, like heroin. One gets hooked on solitude. And in order to feed one's habit one has to relinquish the easy, and I suspect, very comforting intimacy of cohabitation. I use that cumbersome word so as not to exclude those who live together without "benefit of clergy," as Mother would say. I understood there would be numerous small daily rewards were one married to a woman like Catherine. Not that I am one of those disappointed men who mythologize marriage and spend a lifetime regretting they aren't straight. And any time a homosexual puts on his Bernadette-at-the-grotto face and talks reverentially about his "marriage," meaning his present relationship with his current lover, it makes me want to reach for the Rolaids.

"How was your trip to the village? Tell me about my niece. Should I like her?"

"Why shouldn't you? She is far more mature at eighteen than I ever was. Your sister must be doing something right." Catherine emptied something into the sink. "But we had a flurry of excitement. The local bank was robbed."

"The bank?"

"There's only one. It's a small town. Just before closing time three armed men burst in and held the place up. They got away with the payroll for our one big industry, the textile mill."

"That kind of episode barely makes the paper in Montreal."

"I know. That is one of the reasons I prefer living in the country. Here come the young people."

Elizabeth and Robert walked into the kitchen. Her clothing was not in disarray; stray pine needles did not cling to her skirt.

Catherine said something about the weekend being warm; Elizabeth made an observation about the view, just enough dialogue to get them through the kitchen and off stage right.

"How are you coming with the beans?" asked Catherine as she opened the oven door to check on the roast. And aroma of cooked lamb and garlic filled the kitchen.

"Slow and steady wins the race," I said, continuing to snap beans, "although the likelihood of the tortoise actually beating the hare is highly suspect. There's a nasty rumour going around that when the rabbit crossed the finishing line, the tortoise had travelled about eight inches. Hardly worth noticing."

"Oh, I wouldn't say that. At the risk of sounding unladylike, I have always thought eight inches well worth noticing."

I glanced up at Catherine. Although her back was towards me I could see her shoulders shaking. I burst out laughing myself.

"For shame, Catherine Bradford. You bring the blush to my cheek. I shall have to say, 'La, madame!' and hide prettily behind my colander."

She began to slice green pepper. "You know something? No woman is adult until she can laugh at her own sexuality. I remember I could hardly wait for my first period, my first lay, my first baby. But it was the first time I actually found myself laughing at the heavy breathing that I realized I was all grown up. It killed that particular romance. Probably just as well. Every morning he used to tell me at length about his dreams, which sprang from an extraordinarily pedestrian subconscious."

"I have finished the beans. Would you like me to milk the tethered cow, or collect the brown eggs from beneath cross hens with a basket carried daintily in the crook of my arm?"

"Not just now. Make yourself another drink and go out onto

the porch to admire the sunset. It is a house rule that one must admire the sunset."

"Why not?" I replied. "By the way, I am covered, but not dressed. Should I change for dinner?"

"Heavens no! This is the country. I have invited a friend of Dad's to have dinner with us. But she is American and always overdressed."

"You mean I don't have to change into white flannels, blue blazer, old school tie, and white oxfords with black toe caps and heels?"

"Do you even own such garments?"

"No, but I wanted you to realize that I know better."

"Point made. Now off you go to admire, as the French would say, 'the nature.' "

I crossed the thick beige carpet covering the living room floor and went out to the covered porch facing the lake. A sunset was indeed in progress. So far Larry was the sole spectator. The almost full tumbler he held suggested he was either nursing his first drink or had moved into his second. "The weather's here; wish you were lovely," he volunteered.

"What is that old saying? Something about red sky at night, sailor's delight. Red sky in morning, sailor's warning."

"Wrong!" said Larry. "It goes: Red hankie at night, sailor's delight. Red dork in the morning, sailor's warning."

"Somehow, Larry, I don't think that's quite it. Although these days a red sky at night is just as likely to mean your neighbourhood nuclear reactor is melting down."

"Squash a bug; get acid rain!" Larry moved up close. I could tell a confidence was coming on. "Two nights ago," he began, "I had the seventeenth biggest disappointment of my life. I met this psychiatrist, American citizen, but oh so German. I mean *Cherman!* Erich von Stroheim to die. And just the tiniest bit opinionated. One might even stretch a point and say authoritarian . . ."

I turned off my mind. Larry belongs to that particular species of homosexual which gets far more pleasure from the telling of sexual escapades than from the flings themselves. The vicarious experience is more real than the real. And he is worse than Don Giovanni for keeping lists. As most of his stories are junk food for thought, I made a couple of grunts, as though I were listening, and turned my full attention to the sunset, beautiful but dumb.

Mark came out onto the porch, his hair still wet from the shower. "Were you talking about me? My ears are burning."

"Probably a short in your Sony Walkman," I suggested. "Have you come out to enjoy the free sunset?"

"Yes, but it's more beautiful from the shore. You can see the reflection of the sun in the surface of the lake. Want to walk down and take a look?"

"Is one of you stalwart types prepared to carry me back up?" asked Larry.

"No!" Our voices came out in unison.

"Then I'll sit this one out. You can tell me about it."

I followed Mark down the path to the shore. He had been correct, yet again. The ribbon of reflection bisecting the surface of the water was beautiful, almost too beautiful, so obscenely romantic it could have turned me onto the Hunchback of Notre Dame.

"Ta-da!" exclaimed Mark, opening his arms to embrace the view. "Did I lie to you?"

"No, you did not. It pains me to say so, but you did not. Come to think of it you never did lie. Sometimes I wish you had." I walked out to the end of the concrete jetty. "If only the wind was blowing through my hair I could pretend I was the French lieutenant's woman."

Mark came to stand beside me. We looked like twins with our conservative shirts and cotton slacks. Only Mark was wearing jogging shoes, middle-aged bootees. "So what's with the jogging shoes? Do you have to eat and run?"

"Not quite. I'll take you sailing tomorrow, if we get some wind." A large sailboat, possibly a Lightning, anchored about thirty yards from shore sat motionless on the still surface of the lake.

"No, you won't. Sailboats are lovely to watch, boring to ride."

"You'd be surprised. *The Flying Dutchman* is quite a boat."

"*The Flying Dutchman!* You've got to be kidding. Where do you keep Senta, and the eight tiny reindeer?"

Mark groaned.

"Speaking of Senta, let's join hands and leap to our deaths the way she does at the end of the opera. Headline: Died at sunset during sunset years."

"The water is only four feet deep."

"I see. That is a drawback. I guess we are condemned to go on living." I struck my forehead.

He smiled. I wished he hadn't. I wish nobody would smile, ever. Smiles disarm me. To zap someone who is smiling with a zinger is like hitting a little girl wearing glasses who is down.

"You really haven't changed a bit, Geoffry. You still put up a barrage of wisecracks between yourself and truth."

"What is that supposed to mean? And who over fifty wants truth? Certainly not me. I'm like Blanche DuBois. I want Belle Reve and paper lanterns over the bare bulb and della Robbia blue. Truth is like mercury; it can poison the system."

"Lighten up, will you, Geoffry? Which is another way of saying would you please return the head you have just bitten off."

"Jesus, Mark, look at us. Five minutes after you walk into my life after twenty-odd years we're beginning to scrap like a couple of terriers. Do you want to know the truth? Do you want me to tell you how good you still look to me after all these years? Would you like me to say that between the waves lapping at the shore and the light slanting across the lake, and so forth and so on?"

"Yes."

"Well, I won't. I am a middle-aged crank. You are a middle-aged husband. We are both old enough to know better. And I don't want sex in the bushes. If I did, I am quite certain one of those sheepdogs would be more than happy to oblige."

"Neither do I. Certainly not in the bushes anyway. You're right. Our lives have diverged. But at the moment I can't help feeling sorry that they have. I suppose it's the price one pays for being middle-aged."

"And, face it, you *are* middle-aged," I replied crossly. I was cross because I had been touched. First that damn smile, and then an invitation. I had come to the country hoping to survive the weekend, not to fan an old flame. "We are all young in our heads. And now, my dear Mark, to use the oldest exit line in the world, 'I think I need another drink.' "

"Aren't you going to stay and make a wish on a falling satellite?"

"I think not."

As he turned to walk back along the jetty, he laughed. "I thought 'I have a headache' was the oldest."

I joined him in laughter. "That's the second oldest. The third is: 'I think there's someone at the door.' "

VI

When we got back to the house the dinner guest had arrived and was sitting on the porch with Larry and Mr. Bradford, who introduced me to Mrs. Harrington.

"Call me Madge," she said in a whiskey baritone, squeezing my hand.

"How do you do – Madge," I replied, my tongue forming itself uneasily around the name.

Catherine had been right. Madge was American in the same way that Lake Michigan is water. She was overdressed, gloriously so. For an informal dinner in the country she wore a brocade pant-suit over a white lamé blouse, diamond earrings, which even to my unpractised eye looked real, and high-heeled, sling-back pumps. On the redwood patio table, lying beside what looked like bourbon on the rocks, lay a gold mesh evening bag. She must have been the same age as Mr. Bradford, definitely on the winter side of seventy; but she was fighting the good fight with all her might, to which her orange hair, awesome cleavage, and excellent ankles bore witness.

I could tell she and Larry were hitting it off, not surprisingly as she had all the makings of a twenty-four carat fag hag. I picked up my empty glass and went first to the bar. However, instead of returning to the porch I continued on down the hall into the kitchen where Catherine was held hostage.

"Is your hair clinging in damp strands to your forehead? Are there beads of perspiration on your upper lip? Is there aught I can do? I almost mean that."

"Please bring me a scotch and water, no ice."

I complied.

"Did you meet Madge?"

"Yes, I did."

"She comes on a bit like the Rose Bowl Parade, but she's really an interesting woman. You name it; she's done it. She used to be a showgirl."

"As in 'wink, wink, nudge, nudge'? "

"Now, Geoffry, don't jump to conclusions. Just because a girl takes off her clothes in public doesn't mean she does so in private."

"As we say in law, Catherine: a strong presumption."

"She adores Father. I wish he would marry her or go to live with her and stop depending on me." Catherine came to sit across from me at the kitchen table. "Do you suppose I have a heart of stone because I don't want Dad to move in with Mark and me? He really doesn't know what to do with himself since Mother died. And in spite of all his golf and talk of fitness he has a tricky heart. I don't like the idea of his living alone. And he refuses to hire a housekeeper. Am I a deficient daughter?"

"Indeed not. It is only in Victorian novels that five gene-rations of one family live happily together in an eternity of sherry punch and Sunday dinners. I do not for a second believe that being a responsible child means tucking Mum and Dad into bed. My own mother thinks it would be lovely if we lived together. And we could; her apartment is huge. What she doesn't realize is that I would make her miserable. Not that I would beat and abuse her. Nor would I, as my sister would have it, ration her liquor and cigarettes. But my presence, or lack of it, my unwillingness to sit and drink and watch TV and discuss her friends for hours on end, would upset her. To have me under her roof and not have my full attention would be harder for her to accept than not having me there at all. Now I see her when I can, though I couldn't possibly see her often enough. But 'guilt' is a word I eradicated from my vocabulary on my fortieth birthday. End of speech."

Catherine reached across the table and squeezed my hand. "You are an oasis of commonsense in a sea of sentiment. And now I must do something about getting dinner onto the table. Would you ask Mark to come and carve?"

Dinner passed as dinner must, in the large dining room around a long oak refectory table. High on the wall a china-rack circled the room on which Quimper plates and Toby jugs were arranged at regular intervals. Fortunately it was comfortably above eye level. An odd assortment we were, too, enough to put any World War II movie bomber crew to shame. The most immediate item of local news on everybody's mind was the bank robbery. But after ringing the changes on ain't it awful and whatever is the world coming to, the topic petered out. Politics emerged briefly, Mr. Bradford observing that democracy was perhaps an imperfect system, but the best one we had at the moment. It was up to all Canadians to make the system work; a good workman never blames his tools, he concluded, inevitably.

I suggested that the idea of absolute power corrupting absolutely was a fallacy. Absolute power purifies; any absolute is pure. It is having only a little power which corrupts. Consequently democracy fails because the system is organized in a way which allots only a little power to any one person. Ergo: a corrupt system.

Not surprisingly, Larry joined in with an observation which sent the conversation off on a tangent. Everyone in the world is on some sort of power trip, he suggested. Look at the emperor in the fairy tale. He knew perfectly well he wasn't wearing any clothes, new or otherwise. He was a flasher, and being emperor he was the only man in the kingdom who could get away with it.

On the point of ignoring Larry's interruption and illustrating the point I had just made, I broke off, suddenly mindful of the strong Anglo taboo of not contradicting one's elders. The over twenty years separating Mr. Bradford and me rendered his opinion inviolate, at least in public. I was at liberty to think him a fool in the privacy of my thoughts, but these same thoughts must never translate themselves into words.

When I was much younger and still impressionable, I can remember Mother's insisting upon the importance of pulling one's weight in a social situation, as though we were so many dray horses. As a result, all my parents' friends talked endlessly. Nobody ever seemed to listen. To be a mere listener meant you were not pulling your weight, a definite social stigma, like divorce, getting the maid pregnant, or not giving to charity.

As a gesture to Catherine and Mark, I switched subjects completely and asked Mr. Bradford whether May wasn't a bit early for golf. Were the fairways, and particularly the greens, in adequate shape for play? It turned out to be the right wrong question, as Mr. Bradford related, for the benefit of the table at large, the highlights of his game with Mark that morning.

Unfortunately for us, from his very first drive, which he sliced sending the ball into the long grass, the entire game had been one long battle with nature.

It is one thing to play golf. It is another thing to talk about it. The entire eighteen holes had, it would seem, turned out to be a cruel sequence of unplayable lies, sand traps, missed putts, the last naturally due to the inferior condition of the greens. Nor would he, as he took pains to make clear, stoop to the expediency of playing winter rules and teasing the ball into a more favourable position before his swing. The inside of his golf bag was lined with a hair-shirt.

I glanced at Mark. He sat in a trance of boredom looking as though tiny Venetian blinds had been pulled closed over his eyes.

On the eighteenth and final hole the golf cart had mired itself in a gully still marshy from the spring runoff. For several tense seconds it was touch and go as to whether Mr. Bradford would make it up to the green to sink his last, long, triumphant putt.

"Now, Father, don't go boasting," said Catherine, her real reason for interrupting to get the mint sauce into circulation. "Mark always gives you a huge handicap." She then turned her attention to drawing out Elizabeth who, along with Robert, had materialized seemingly out of nowhere just as the roast was being carried to table.

In reply to a question about the other members of her family, Elizabeth let drop that her younger sister intended becoming an elementary school teacher. Madge picked up on the remark and launched into a tale of how she once had occasion to visit a progressive kindergarten where her niece taught.

"You should have seen the place," Madge continued. "Run up to the nines. Broadloom all over the walls and moulded fibreglass furniture. Not your little red schoolhouse by a long shot. My niece was in charge of the babies, and is she a pain in the wazoo. She stood there like a Moonie telling us" – here Madge made her voice go plummy – "how she discouraged traditional games, like musical chairs or tag, games of exclusion. She did not believe any child should be 'it' or 'out.' "

Madge paused for a swallow of bourbon; it was evident she never touched wine. The last rays of light sneaking in through the dining room window bounced off the huge, rectangular topaz on her fourth finger.

"Instead the Munchkins played Toesies, pressing the soles of their feet together as they rolled over and over. Some played Sticky Popcorn, pretending they were just that and grabbing each other just about everywhere in the process. I cut out before the demonstration of Bump and Scoot, a variation of tag where everyone is 'it.' "

"Sounds a bit like *Brave New World*," said Mark, who up to now had been silent. "The supervised erotic play for children."

"When I was a child," I began, immediately regretting the tiresome observation, "back at a time when sex was dirty and the air was clean, we sneaked off to the garage to play doctor. It may have been clandestine, but at least we were not assaulted by porno mags at the candy store."

"I never buy pornography," interrupted Larry, "because I don't have a pornograph." There followed a pause. Puns do have a way of bringing conversations to a grinding halt.

By the time the social juices had begun to flow again, Mark began to pull his weight, expounding on both the pleasures and disadvantages of country living. From Robert came a reminiscence of a tennis game where he had pulled a tendon but still managed to limp his way to victory and a silver-plated trophy.

"Has everyone finished?" asked Catherine in a hostessy voice, pushing her tone up nearly an octave. The artifice compelled attention. Mumbled assurances that nobody wanted any more brought Robert and Elizabeth to their feet to clear the table. They both moved with careful deliberation, their faces expressionless, their gestures unhurried. I strongly suspected they had smoked a joint while the rest of us sophisticates had been belting back the liquor.

Elizabeth handed around the spinach salad while Catherine explained that the only lettuce in the stores was tired iceberg from California and that it was still too early for local produce. I confess that I found the idea of spinach salad without quiche refreshing.

Mr. Bradford refused the salad. Then he uttered the dread word: bridge. It tolled like a knell.

Larry put down his napkin, squared his shoulders, and announced to the table that he and Madge would take on any couple who had the temerity to accept the challenge. That left four adults, all of whom could be called but only two chosen. I sat very still and pretended hard that I was invisible. It was decided that Catherine and her father would pick up the gauntlet. So pleased was I at being let off the hook that I suggested they begin the game right away while I cleared the table. I also assured Robert and Elizabeth that Mark and I could easily manage, as they were obviously anxious to go out.

As I am an infrequent houseguest I seldom have occasion to observe first hand the daily nuts and bolts routine of household

operation, such as the wife unpacking groceries or making dinner. I was surprised and amazed at how handy Mark had become
around the kitchen. Marriage appeared to have domesticated
him, and in short order we had the remains of dinner filed
away. I really did not mind helping. It had the charm of novelty.
And I had not been obliged to lie my way out of bridge.

Mark opened the kitchen door and called the dogs into the
house for the night because of nocturnal skunks. Soon, he explained, the dogs would be clipped for the summer months, and
giving them a bath in tomato juice to kill the skunk odour was
less of an undertaking. The dogs greeted us as though we had
just returned from the North Pole. Much better, I decided,
than a pair of Dobermann pinschers who want to take off the
arm at the elbow. Each sheepdog grabbed one of my hands in
his mouth, exerting no pressure, and telling me what a fine
fellow I really was. I endured in silence, I am always dumb to
kind animals.

Mark dismissed me, saying he would finish up and join me
on the porch shortly. The way lay past the bar. What the hell,
I thought, pouring myself a highball even though I do not as a
rule drink after dinner. I passed the bridge table, as self-con-
tained and sealed off from the outside world as if encased in a
plastic bubble. Madge took a swallow of bourbon, gave a squawk,
and suggested maybe Larry had overbid. Larry grinned boyishly
and said he knew she could do it. Catherine looked glum, and
her father sat back, wearing the long-suffering look of a serious
bridge player confronted by those who have the bad manners
to play for fun.

I went to my room and pulled on a sweater, grey, crew-
necked, terminally preppy, then went out onto the porch to sit.

Darkness had fallen; not even the branches were visible. Only a few moments ago they had been large strokes of calligraphy outlined against a pale sky.

I sat shrouded in darkness, sipping my drink, and thinking about Mark, something I had rigorously avoided during dinner. I always have an uneasy feeling that when I am thinking thoughts inappropriate to a situation I will somehow give myself away. To extrapolate from what my mother might have said: if one must think about former lovers at all, do so in private, never at the dinner table. But it was hard to avoid looking at Mark during dinner, the few times he spoke. What a handsome man he had become, his natural distinction honed and refined by the passage of time. At the same time he did not have the eight-by-ten glossy look of the matinee idol. To think he was my host, married to Catherine. And here we all were, over twenty years later. Older, I did not doubt, but wiser? The next couple of days would answer that one. I put my mind into neutral; gradually it drifted into reverse . . . .

Mark and I had climbed out of bed the evening after we met and began in earnest to have an affair. After hours of silent sex we suddenly began to talk, to talk as if, like Adam and Eve, we had just discovered that things had names. A creek swelled by spring thaw, our words tumbled out as we both, in the act of telling each about the other, tried at the same time to define ourselves to ourselves.

In retrospect it is easy to see how much we were products of our time. Even though we shared a ravenous sexual hunger for one another, we still had to pretend that we were using only a part of our total sexuality, which is another way of saying that to be bisexual was acceptable, homosexual not. I had been married; Mark had just broken off an extended liaison with an older woman.

Once we established that having sex with other men was an option, not an obsession, we embarked on one of those sexually charged, romantically slanted relationships where every breath is monitored, every word scrutinized, every look misconstrued. What we both wanted was a relationship of granite permanence but conceived as perpetual honeymoon. We steered an uneven course between what I like to think of as the Scylla of society and the Charybdis of our own self-consciousness on an odyssey of misunderstanding.

Mark was touchy about his image, his concept of himself before the world. Naked, he was pagan; dressed, a middle-of-the-road Anglican, drearier than which there is nothing under the sun. It goes almost without saying that much of his self-image rested on a firm foundation of male chauvinist piggery.

Men could cook, but they did not do dishes. Men did not sew. Mark would beat a path to the tailor to have the designer label stitched back onto his tie. Men did not do laundry. On more than one occasion tempers flared when we were ready to check out of a hotel, and the socks and underwear he had solemnly sent out for washing had not been returned, particularly if I suggested he didn't keep his underwear on long enough for it to get dirty. He wouldn't even use the washing machine in his apartment building.

Finally, women were not to be treated as equals. I do not think men and women should sit down and arm wrestle over a bottle of beer, nor do I believe a woman has to be escorted down in the elevator and put into the waiting cab, particularly when she came directly from work to the party unaided. But

Mark was forever lighting cigarettes, fetching drinks, positioning ashtrays, as if females were a bit simpleminded. I suggested more than once that all this cavalier attention was dishonest because it could be misinterpreted as something other than reflex politeness.

We never gave all-male parties. I think a pride of pansies or a gaggle of faggots can be pretty wearing; one tires of constant camp. But Mark withdrew to the point of catatonia when surrounded by les girls, particularly as about eighty per cent of any group of them tried to put the make on him. He was unbelieveably good-looking. Not that I was jealous. Jealousy springs from insecurity, and whatever doubts I may have tried to hide they did not include any real worry that Mark might find someone more interesting than I, at least not at that kind of party.

It worked for a while, our charade of being just a couple of bachelors, chumming around on the loose, surrounded by lots of women, although no one in particular. Whether anyone was really fooled no longer matters. It didn't matter then, although I could not have convinced Mark in order to save my quasi-immortal soul . . . .

"Is this seat taken?" asked Mark, who had come out of the house so silently I did not hear him.

"Are you a masher?" I said, trying to keep it light.

"Not on weekends. Now, as your host, it is my duty, my pleasant duty, to entertain you. The bridge game will continue for a while, although I suspect Catherine and Mr. Bradford – why do you suppose I still call him that? – are being sorely tried by their partners. Would you like to watch television?"

"No, thanks. For some irrational reason I still think of television as an urban pastime."

"So, how have you been, Geoffry, in terms of the broad canvas?"

"The broad canvas? My life has been quite small-scale of late, really. Very little broad sweep or blazing colour. On the plus side, I don't wear a pacemaker; I still have all my teeth; I don't have cancer, at least not yet; and my firm has all the work it can handle. I really can't complain, but I do, constantly. And you?"

"I see your façade is still very much intact. You always used to remind me of a toffee apple, hard on the outside, soft on the inside."

"And rotten at the core. Tell me about you and Catherine."

"We are both very well, as you can see. We seem to have gone against the traffic moving in from Ontario back to Quebec. And, as you probably know, it was a second marriage for both of us. We weren't old, but we weren't getting any younger. And we never stopped thinking of Quebec as home."

As we sat there in the cool impersonal darkness, the voices from the bridge table barely audible, I had an overpowering urge to reach over and touch Mark in order to push back the stark realization that so many years had slipped by so quickly and with so little to show. But I was afraid the gesture would be misunderstood.

Mark spoke. "I don't mean to pry, and you can tell me to mind my own business, but have you been happy with the way you chose to live your life?"

"If I were to object, Mark, it would not be to your question but to the mush-minded idea of happiness as a criterion for anything. 'Life, liberty, and the pursuit of happiness.' Pursue and you will never find. No, I have not been happy. At times I have enjoyed a degree of contentment. What I suppose you really mean is am I sorry I did not marry again. Yes and no. I would have gained some things, lost out on others. I would have met with problems, different ones perhaps, but problems nonetheless. It is naïve and immature to imagine that the road not taken is any better or worse than the one we took."

"I suppose you're right. But then you always were a bit of a cynic."

"Oh, for Christ's sake, Mark. I'm not a cynic just because I don't happen to believe Ken and Barbie lived happily ever after. I'm simply not a fool, that's all."

"You city folks sure tell it like it is. One more question?"

"Yes. I don't promise to answer it, but ask away."

"Did you ever meet . . . anyone else?"

"Hundreds of times, and each love truer than that of the night before." I tried to sound flippant, but his question nettled me.

"You've slept with a lot of people?"

"In a manner of speaking. I generally try to stay awake."

"But was there . . . anyone in particular?"

"You're nailing me, aren't you? Yes, I suppose there was. In spite of the smarts I like to think I have, I got mixed up with a married man. Geoffry Chadwick: boy bimbo. There isn't much to tell. Most affairs seem distressingly alike, especially when they are over."

"Did you remain friends?"

The question surprised me. I bought time by taking a couple of sips of my highball. "I suppose you could say we did. We are still on speaking terms, whatever that means. I saw him only last . . . only recently. But since we separated, he has moved to the west coast and gone native: sex and drugs and rock and roll. It is not a scene I find interesting. We no longer seem to have much in common."

"Do you think you and I do?"

I was not certain what Mark was getting at precisely, but I played it straight, and safe. "We certainly do: Catherine. In our own different ways we are both very devoted to her. One thing I always did admire about you, Mark, was your taste. And I have to admit your taste in wives is impeccable. Now would you believe my glass is empty?"

I escaped to the bar. If anyone had told me this morning that before midnight I would be telling the first man I had ever really loved about the only other man I really loved, I would probably have uttered a rude word. And even though there was a bottle of scotch already open I cracked the seal on my own bottle of Black Label. I owed it to myself.

By virtue of the ancient military tactic of divide and conquer, Larry and Madge carried the day, or evening, as it were, and won three rubbers in a row. As Larry poured them both a victory drink it was evident that Catherine and her father were on cool terms. Chilly night air finally drove Mark indoors. We all had a nightcap while Mark and I tried to sweeten the aftermath of defeat. Bridge is really a dreadful game, the cause of more divorces than wife beating.

Not surprisingly, Mr. Bradford was the first to head off to bed, pleading an early golf game on the morrow. Shortly afterwards Madge, who seemed to be one of those people on whom liquor has no noticeable effect, said the customary thank yous and goodnights. Larry walked her out to the car. I happened to spot the gold evening bag on the coffeetable. "She's left her bag," I said, "I'll take it out to her."

I had no sooner spoken than the vehicle crunched past the door and up the gravel driveway.

"Too late," said Catherine. "She always leaves her keys in the ignition. This is the country, after all. One of us will drop off the bag tomorrow."

The four of us sat for a while longer, chatting about nothing in particular. Mark took the dogs outside for one last pee, then announced that country folks turned in early. Although I was not particularly sleepy I too made going-to-bed noises in order not to be trapped by Larry into at least three more nightcaps. Predictably he poured himself another drink and settled down in the glassed-in sunporch to which the television set had been banished. Lights were left burning for Elizabeth and Robert, who would no doubt be late, and in short order a calm descended on the house.

The quiet was so profound as to be almost unnerving. City night is filled with reassuring noises; city air has texture; harmful, no doubt, but addictive. I popped a couple of aspirins to counteract the highballs I had drunk after dinner and then undressed, self-consciously not looking at my naked body in the full-length mirror bolted to the closet door. Downward mobility is more than just a social phenomenon.

I got into bed, erased my mind of thought, and almost to my surprise began to feel drowsy. I thought about moving my left arm into a more comfortable position, but the effort seemed too great. I drifted away.

I must at some point have been dreaming a vivid dream, for I woke suddenly with a feeling of disorientation. Feeling around on the night-table I located the light switch on the duck decoy lamp and consulted my watch: three A.M. Through the wall I could hear Larry's regular snores. He dislikes being reminded of his snoring, a macho activity of extreme bad taste. He would like to believe only straight men snore, but when drunk he sounds like a pneumatic drill.

I switched off the light and lay in the dark trying to decide whether to rouse myself sufficiently to read or just to wait out the hours until sleep decided to return. And like someone who has recently stopped smoking and tries not to think about a cigarette, I found my thoughts turning again and again towards Mark, asleep upstairs . . . .

We had stayed together for over two years, hacking our way through an emotional jungle with verbal machetes. We had started to see one another for pleasure and to our mutual astonishment, stumbled into passion. I have always found it curious how so many people seem to long for a deep, romantic involvement. To me it is like longing for cholera or gout. Passion is not a condition; it is a form of temporary insanity.

We arose each morning, our nerve ends stripped to the waist, prepared to throw ourselves headlong against the barbed wire of imaginary slights and broken glass of non-existent offences. If I had to work late at the office he took it to mean I really didn't want to see him. If he had dinner with his family I felt he only wanted a free night so he could go out to the bars. Accusations and counter accusations flew back and forth. The only way we seemed to be able to reconcile differences was by going to bed. We lived in a constant state of sexual white heat, the natural chemical attraction polarized by the catalyst of insecurity, that by-product of so-called true love. The more we loved one another the more we sank into doubt and recrimination. It was a total goddamn mess.

We never seriously thought of separating. We couldn't, manacled as we were by something we could not begin to understand. But it was not all bad. There were moments, notably as we lay together in the aftermath of lovemaking, our bodies touching, our tongues silent, when I had the feeling of transcendence that love can sometimes bring, but seldom does.

Then the moment passed and tensions began to flare. Initially Mark did not have as much experience as I in verbal sparring, but he turned out to be a ready pupil. He was touchy to the point of paranoia over how he imagined the two of us were seen by others.

"By the way," he said one afternoon, swinging his legs over the side of the bed, "you know I would prefer you not to use en-dearments in public."

"I don't."

"Yesterday at the Bradys you called me 'dollink.' "

"Dollink is hardly an endearment."

"It depends on the context. 'Darling' by any other name is an endearment, especially when used between to men. By the same token I would prefer not to be called 'Sweetheartburn' or 'Behated one.' "

"Ever hear of irony, meathead?"

"Yes, I've heard of irony. The fact remains my name is Mark; yours, Geoffry. Why can't we use them? I don't enjoy being called 'Sugar Substitute,' 'Tawdry Treasure,' or 'Cher Maître.' And I particularly dislike 'sir or madame.' "

"How about 'To Whom It May Concern'?" I asked, covering myself with a sheet.

"How about Mark, plain Mark. Not Saint Mark. Just Mark."

"Jesus, you're dreary."

"Maybe I'd better go."

"You're pouting. Men called Mark don't pout. 'Darling Angels' pout, but not he-men." I made my voice go deep and gruff. "Besides, ever since you started smoking that pipe, that big butch briar, haven't you noticed how women cross their legs nervously when you enter a room? And you've taken to walking into crowded rooms in that mock-male fashion, as though you had just sprained your knees or wet your pants. No one will ever blow your cover." I made the mistake of laughing out loud. "Now why don't you just come back to bed. I'll pretend I'm Little Red Riding Hood's grandmother and you can be the big bad wolf and eat me up. Yum."

"You're really not funny, Geoffry. If I've asked you once, I've asked you a hundred times . . ."

"Eighty-seven, to be precise."

"I think maybe I'll leave."

"I thought we were going to the movies."

"Go by yourself."

"But what if a big nasty man comes and sits beside me and puts his hand on my knee and offers me a Babe Ruth candy bar and takes me back to his hotel room and makes me do dirty and shameful things? And it will all be your fault, my Not-So-Funny Valentine."

By this time he was pulling on his trousers. He had already put on his long-suffering expression, his mouth compressed into a straight line.

"Oh, for Christ's sake, Mark – excuse me, Mr. Crosby. If I promise, solemnly, cross my heart and hope to die, couldn't you find it in your heart to forgive me?"

"Geoffry, you are a real pain in the ass."

"You weren't saying that fifteen minutes ago. And now it's your turn in the saddle."

We fell silent; I sat up and pounded the pillows. "Jesus, Mary, and Joseph, Mark, stop giving me that brown-eyed, long-suffering stare. You look like Elsie, the Borden cow."

That was definitely the wrong thing to have said, as evidence of which I went to the movies alone . . . .

On the point of sitting up and pounding my pillows, more from impatience than to make them more comfortable, I thought I heard a footstep in the kitchen. I listened hard. Sure enough, someone had just shut the refrigerator door. By now awake, I decided to investigate.

I got out of bed, pulled on my robe, and opened my bedroom door. A light had been turned on in the kitchen. Five steps brought me there.

"Catherine, isn't it a little past your bed time?"

"Oh dear, I hope I didn't wake you."

"No, a dream did that. Are you sneaking about the house like the crazy wife in *Jane Eyre*, laughing shrilly and setting fire to the bed curtains?"

"Not yet. For some reason I woke up and couldn't get back to sleep. Will you join me for a glass of milk?"

"I guess one wouldn't hurt."

"How about something to eat?"

"A lobster soufflé would be nice."

"So would a bowl of cereal. Or a piece of apple pie. Lots of lemon? Very little sugar? I baked it myself."

I smiled and shook my head to indicate no thanks. "And she bakes too! Believe it or not, I have a huge respect for the domestic arts. I tried to bake a pie once. I put four and twenty blackbirds under the crust, and when I went to cut it open they were all dead, and their feathers were burnt and singed. Not a dainty dish to set before a king, or a queen for that matter. Did the teeny boppers get home? Or do I start to wring my hands?"

Catherine poured two glasses of milk and sat down across from me at the pine table. "Bob's car is in the driveway. And I think I heard Elizabeth moving around in her room."

"Have you recovered from the bridge game?"

Catherine made a small gesture of impatience. "Isn't Father the limit? A game of bridge is just that, a game. But he carries on as though it were the Battle of Waterloo. I really don't much like cards; I only played to be accommodating, as Mark gets very impatient playing with Dad. Poor old Pop. He wants to move in with us so badly."

"What do you think the chances are he will marry Mrs. Thingummy – Madge?"

"I don't know. I know he likes her. But deep down he thinks her common."

"On the contrary, I think she is very uncommon. I've met dozens of women who went to better private schools, but she is the first, to my knowledge, who has been a showgirl. And she's pretty jazzy. I think she'd make a wonderful wicked step-mother."

Catherine smiled. "She would indeed. By the way, I hadn't realized you and Mark already knew each other."

Her question seemed totally matter of fact, and I feigned a casualness I did not feel. "A long time ago, and never very well. We lost touch when he moved up to Toronto. Are you happy with him, Catherine, as they say in women's movies?"

"I guess so."

"Then please don't tell me about it. If there is one thing I can't stand it's other people's happiness. I dislike it even more than other people's success."

Catherine laughed out loud. "In that case, he makes me miserable. He beats me and runs around with other women. Worse still, he squeezes the toothpaste from the top of the tube."

As Catherine spoke I studied her carefully without seeming to. Hair tousled from sleep, face innocent of makeup, her tall figure knotted into a quilted housecoat, she struck me as the kind of woman one would be pleased to wake up beside.

"To tell the awful truth, Geoffry, Mark is very good to me. He treats me right, as the songs used to say. More important, he gives me room to breathe. It's just that . . . at the risk of sounding dreadfully adolescent, I wonder if we all don't ask ourselves once in a while if there isn't something out there that we are missing."

"There most certainly is. What most people fail to realize is that whatever it might be is seldom any more interesting or more worthwhile than what we actually have."

"The chill wind of commonsense. Do you want to know something funny? After all these years I guess it can be told. I cried at your wedding, not in that soppy way that women cry at weddings, but because my heart was absolutely, irreversibly broken."

"What do you mean?"

"Susan married you and I didn't."

"She did you an enormous favour, Catherine. Believe me."

She smiled into my eyes. "I don't doubt it for a second. But I had an awful crush on you."

"Would you have had your awful crush had I not been engaged

to your cousin?"

"Most probably not. The mere fact that you were unattainable made you ten times as attractive. And we all know youth loves to be unhappy."

"But there are happy endings, Catherine. You have married, successfully it would seem, for a second time. I, on the other hand, have reverted to being a testy bachelor."

"But less unattainable, one would like to think. And you have just given me a delightful whiff of naughtiness. When was I last in a compromising situation? When did I last sit around in my nightgown at three-thirty A.M. with a scantily clad man who was not my husband."

"Last weekend, as a matter of fact. You used dinner with your father as an alibi, but I wasn't fooled for a second."

Again Catherine laughed out loud. "Geoffry, you're impossible." She reached across the table and laid her hand lightly on mine. Her touch was warm. "But, dammit, it's good to see you again after all these years." She stood. "Now off we go to our respective kips so we will be fresh and rested for another day of fun and frolic in the country. I'll turn off the lights. Sleep well."

To my astonishment I did.

VII

I was just floating up towards the surface of consciousness when a knock sounded at my door. Before I could say "Come in," the door opened and Larry, fully dressed, poked his head inside.

"It's me: star of stage, screen, and latrine. What do Popeye the Sailor and a Greek chef have in common?"

"Why don't you come all the way in so I can strike you?" I pulled the sheet up over my face.

"Give up? They both eat Olive Oil."

"Larry, I guess you'll have to do until Sleazy comes along. What's it like out?"

"I don't know. I don't have it out."

"Make yourself useful and raise the blind."

Larry gave the shade a yank. With a life of its own it slipped from his hand, shot upwards, and spun around the roller with a loud slapping sound. He shrugged and came to sit on the edge of the bed. "Chadwick, I need you to tell me how we are going to get through the day. I had no idea this place was so isolated. I mean my idea of the country is Rosedale. I'll bet they don't even have a dirty-bookmobile."

"We are about to join Bucolics Anonymous. Now, leave and shut the door. I shall arise and go now, into the bathroom. By the way, it will probably be a longish day. I suggest you hold off drinking until noon."

"Will Big Sister be watching me?"

"You got it. Now beat it."

I shut myself into the bathroom. As I was combing my hair I noticed a wooden plaque on the wall, hanging above the toilet. I lifted it off. A large slab of walnut or maple, it resembled a chopping board with a handle through which a hole had been drilled. Four small brass screws attached a square of enamelled copper on which a poem had been painstakingly inscribed.

> *Kleenex, matches, pins & strings,*
> *Filter tips & other things,*
> *Country plumbing will reject,*
> *So, Urbanite, be circumspect.*
> *It's all a bother & a care,*
> *But oh - my dear - so necessaire!*

Another grim hostess present.

As I showered, the shower curtain managed to wrap its clammy self around my legs, but I persevered. I tried not to think of my own bathroom, sliding glass doors for the shower, water which remained at a constant temperature, not whimsically alternating between scalding and frigid, and acres of counter space on which to put my toilet articles.

By the time I loomed in the kitchen door Catherine, still in her housecoat, was standing at the stove making pancakes for Larry. She smiled at me. "Hi, Toots."

"Goodwife Bradford," I began, "when I was a boy the maid wore a coloured uniform to serve breakfast."

"Did she sleep in and put out?" asked Larry who was seated, knife and fork held vertically, napkin tucked under his chin.

"Come and kiss me good morning on my bee-stung lips,"

said Catherine.

"O.K., Blondie."

"Terrific!" exclaimed Larry. "It's going to be just like a Russian play I once saw. Can you believe? It wasn't by Chekhov. Anyhow, they're all marooned on this country estate and everybody falls in love with everybody else out of sheer boredom."

"Sounds like Turgenyev: *A Month in the Country*."

"That's it."

"But remember, Larry, boredom is really a judgement of self on self."

By way of reply Larry made a rude gesture with his fork.

"Where is everybody?" I asked.

"Mark has gone off to show some people a house. Robert and Elizabeth have not yet surfaced. Father left early for nine holes of golf. And as soon as I make you some breakfast, I'll run into town for a few things."

"You're a regular shopping moll. If anyone calls, I'll tell him you are at better stores everywhere. And I never eat breakfast. Only coffee thanks." Catherine poured me a cup.

"Would you pick me up a newspaper?" I asked. "It's silly, I know, but I have to have my little fix of news, especially on weekends."

"I listened to the the radio," Catherine set a plate of pancakes and sausages in front of Larry who tucked in. Being able to eat first thing in the morning links man to the baser creatures. "Nothing much to report. The bank robbers are still at large, which means they are hiding out somewhere. The weather is to continue fine. Now if you'll excuse me I'll go and change."

I sat silent, drinking my black coffee and, in the process, doing inestimable harm to my system. Larry was too busy eating to talk. Not that there was anything I really wanted to say.

After finishing his breakfast Larry stood, stretched, burped. "Maybe there's something to be said for country living, after all. At least when I woke up this morning I didn't have to mastur-bate to get my heart started."

"Do you suppose this could be the thin edge of the wedge?" I asked from the stove as I refilled my cup. I was pleased to see Catherine used cups and saucers, not great clunky, sincere, hand-made mugs which require two hands to lift and which keep the coffee hot for days. "You'll be jogging before you know it."

"And end up with jogger's nipple? Not on your life. I'm off to watch cartoons on the telly. Nothing too taxing. There are flowerbeds, and someone might ask me to pull a weed or some-thing. You know what they say: You can lead a horse to water but you can't lead a horticulture." Larry went onto the sunporch. I don't think he has cracked a book since the advent of television.

I finished my coffee and went outside. The day promised fine. Sunlight dappled the driveway, and the entire landscape wore that particular shade of yellow-green which is the hall-mark of early summer. By landscape I refer of course to those few open spaces which have been cleared of trees. The Quebec landscape, outside of arable land, is trees. Not copses or shaws or thickets, but great ragged stands of cedar, pine, spruce, and the ubiquitous maple. Forests, not woods. Enter at your peril, and turn your ankle in a hole camouflaged by pine needles; or accidentally kick a rotten stump which turns out to be a condo-minium for cross wasps.

I paused dutifully to notice the art nouveau crocus dotting the flowerbeds on either side of the front door, so if challenged later I could admit to having admired the garden. I had not yet been able to ascertain whether my host and hostess were serious gardeners. I hoped not. People who garden are even more ruthless than those who carry photographs of grandchildren, especially when one is on the spot; however, no ornamental urns, concrete planters, wooden tubs, or radial tires filled with soil were to be seen.

A few dandelions dotted the lawn. In spite of what gardeners say, I confess I find it difficult to think of dandelions as weeds. I love their brilliant chrome yellow, definitely macho, as are their spiky leaves and devil-may-care attitude about where they sow themselves. And what in nature is more beautiful than the circular puff of a dandelion gone to seed during those fragile seconds before a casual breeze breaks the perfection.

I set off to explore the grounds, several acres, at least. I was alone, the dogs having barked to be taken along in the back seat of Catherine's station-wagon. About two hundred yards from the house stood a garage in front of which the driveway described a circle where a car could turn easily for the trip back up the road.

Having no particular purpose in mind I set off to look inside. It soon became evident the garage had a variety of uses, the least of which was to house a car. A lawn roller, a wheelbarrow, two bags of golf clubs strapped to frames on wheels, along with assorted garden tools rested at random under the peaked roof. A flight of narrow wooden steps at the rear end of the garage led to what was obviously an upper floor. Curiosity drew me towards the stairs. I don't really suppose having a look at the attic of a country garage could be called snooping, but I found myself nonetheless treading softly on the stairs, my footsteps made soundless by rubber-soled shoes.

The steps led up to a small landing from which one could see the second floor. The place had once been used as servants' quarters, to which a small handbasin at the top of the stairs bore witness. Dominating the odds and bits of furniture was a large sleigh bed. In the bed, fast asleep, lay Catherine's son Robert and my niece Elizabeth.

I beat a hasty retreat, heading back towards the lake. I was furious, not because they were sleeping together but because I had caught them. If Elizabeth wanted to screw around the last thing in the world I wanted was to know about it. To be honest, I was angry with myself. Why had I gone snooping up those stairs in the first place? Larry, damn him, had been right. I could not help chuckling to myself when I thought of how I had told my sister that I would make a lousy chaperone.

I stood on the shoreline watching a light breeze crease the surface of the lake. Warmed by the sun, I pulled off my sweater and fastened it around my waist by knotting the sleeves.

"This seems to be your favourite spot," said Mark's voice behind my back. I turned to see him standing on the grass bordering the beach.

"Just soaking up the solitude before I address myself to being the perfect guest. Did you make a sale?"

"Very likely. They seemed interested. I think the property is overvalued, so I'm trying to get them a better price. But, as they say, a fool and his money are soon parted."

"I have always wondered how a fool and his money got together in the first place."

Mark came to stand beside me. Most middle-aged people are well-advised to avoid direct sunlight, especially in the morning.

That hard, uncompromising light throws every line, pore, pouch, wart, capillary into hard-edged relief. Double chins swell in direct sunlight; bald spots positively twinkle. It only made me crosser to see how well Mark survived the scrutiny of the sun.

"Geoffry," he began, "it turns out I have to go into Montreal, on business. I was wondering if you could give me a lift in on Monday afternoon, or whenever you decide to leave."

"How will you get back?"

"I'll take the bus. Once I get to Montreal a car is more of a liability than an asset. I can always stay with Catherine's father." He laughed, just a bit self-consciously. "Unless you could give me a narrow cot."

"Mark, stop right there. You're not going to Montreal for business, but the business. My apartment, a couple of drinks, a feeling of removal from your own surroundings, and zap! It's too pat, Mark. And you know it."

"Don't you trust me, Geoffry?"

"I don't trust myself. What I must do therefore is to avoid a possible situation. I will drive you to Montreal, if you wish. I will drop you at your father-in-law's apartment."

"What you are saying is that given the opportunity . . ."

"Given the opportunity there is no telling what might happen. Were you unhappily married to a shrew, I might feel different. But I have known Catherine far longer than I have known you. Furthermore I think the world of her. For me to get involved with her husband would be tacky. And you know as well as I do that getting into bed is the easy part. It's getting out that presents problems. We wouldn't be prepared to settle for once overnight. Things would escalate. You would find more excuses to come to Montreal. And we would begin that whole

round of deception and deceit which is ultimately so de-
meaning. And for what? We're too old to recapture the rapture.
It's unfortunate, but it's true. If we once had incandescence we
could only hope to fan a few embers. And at the cost of one in
the eye for Catherine."

"Boy-oh-boy," said Mark softly. "You haven't lost the knack
for making me feel crummy."

"I don't mean to. We can't help the way we feel. What we
can do is monitor our conduct." I made a gesture, palms upward.

"The problem, Geoffry, is that you're right, you tiresome old
bugger."

Unsure of what to do next he punched my shoulder. It was
his way of touching me without being overtly affectionate. I
reached out and put my hand on his arm, and for just a moment
he covered my hand with his. Then, wordlessly, we made our
way up to the house.

I spent the next hour or so browsing through books, with which
the house was generously stocked. It was pleasant: a chapter
here, a couple of pages there. I perused a collection of short
stories which proclaimed themselves post-modernist, whatever
that means. They turned out to be reflective essays in the best
nineteenth-century tradition. Nothing ever really changes. I
read a poem, one with no rhyme scheme nor any perceptible
rhythm, but I did try. It told of how women were moving to a
far country while men watched impassively from the windows
of high towers. I returned the book to the shelf.

At some point, Elizabeth and Robert appeared, said good
morning, and disappeared into the kitchen. I was by this time

amused at how Elizabeth sought to cover her tracks, having taken jeans and a sweater up to the garage room with her so as not to appear in the morning wearing the same clothes she had gone out in last night. With a mother like Mildred one would have to learn subterfuge in order to survive.

A crunch of wheels on gravel followed by excited barks as the dogs spilled from the car, announced the arrival of Catherine. I went into the now empty kitchen, Elizabeth and Robert having taken their coffee outside. Catherine came in through the kitchen door carrying a bag of groceries and a newspaper. From her arm dangled a hard straw handbag with a piece of scrimshaw set into the top. After putting everything down on the counter and pushing her sunglasses up into her hair, she turned to me and struck an attitude with both hands crossed at her throat.

"Did you miss me, dearest?"

With my arms I made a sem-arabesque. "Desperately."

"Good!" She turned to the groceries and lifted out two large tins of tomato juice. "I think the occasion cries out for a bloody Mary."

"Such a hostess! Catherine, if you have a large jug, lemons, Worcestershire sauce, pepper and salt, I will make up a sumptuous batch of mix."

"No tabasco," said Larry, who had materialized in the doorway.

Catherine fetched the required ingredients, plus an Ittala frosted jug. "Shall I make some hors d'oeuvres?"

"That depends," I replied. "Back where I come from hors d'oeuvres fall into one of three categories. A: pretzels or salted nuts, which make you thirstier and cause you to drink more.

B: a block of cheese or pâté, biscuits on the side, strictly do-it-yourself. C: a Ritz cracker, a slice of tomato, a dab of mayo, topped by either a smoked oyster or a rolled anchovy, fish at its most unbuttoned . . ."

"Chadwick," interrupted Larry, "you sure know how to be the life of the party."

"You underestimate me," replied Catherine. "How about hot cheese what-nots, maybe topped with a bit of crisp bacon."

"Well, perhaps."

"Enough idle chat," announced Larry. "Let's get down to some serious drinking."

VIII

I had a feeling of time arrested as I slouched down in one of
the armchairs facing the fireplace, sipping my bloody
Mary, which I had to admit tasted delicious, a little reward
from God for good behaviour. I had been here almost
twenty-four hours. The way I had it figured some time after
lunch on Monday I could make going home gestures. Forty-
eight hours more; one down and two to go. It could have been
a whole lot worse.

Catherine, Mark, Larry, and I all sat around the room looking
like characters from the Chekhov play about those three sisters
who never did get to Moscow. Robert had received an invitation
to a barbecue from somewhere across the lake and telephoned
the hostess to ask if he might bring Elizabeth. Having returned
from golf, Mr. Bradford had gone upstairs to change.

Mark suggested we sit outside; he could fetch lawn chairs from
the garage. I counter-suggested I would rather be inside looking
out than outside looking in, and that folding lawn chairs were
never very comfortable. Catherine agreed with me. Larry rose
and carried his half-empty glass to the bar. He returned with a
full tumbler, and I suspected he had made up the difference with
vodka, not tomato juice. Catherine went out to the kitchen to
rescue her cheese and bacon snacks. The invisible clock ticked on.

The sound of wheels crunching on the driveway caught our
attention.

"One of the problems of living in the country," began Mark, "is that people feel free to drop in unannounced."

He had barely finished his sentence when three men burst through the front door. All I could remember, as I tried to re-collect those first moments, is that they were armed. Two carried what looked like pistols; I know nothing about firearms. The third carried a large gun, possibly a Magnum, although I didn't think that particular weapon existed outside of the movies. He also wore dark glasses whose lenses were mirrors.

"Please don't anybody move," he said very quietly.

The sound of a door banging shut came from the kitchen. With excited barks Grendel and Caliban tore down the pas-sageway towards the living room. The man wearing the glasses spun around and emptied his gun into the astonished animals. With one accord they fell, twitched, whimpered, and lay still.

The three of us in the living room went rigid with shock. For a second I tried to convince myself that I was in the middle of a ghastly dream, that any second I would awaken, sweating, in the reassuring warmth of my own bed. The noise brought Cathe-rine running down the hall.

"Oh – my god," she said softly as she caught sight of the two dead dogs and the three armed men.

"Get in here," said the one wearing the glasses, in his quiet, almost off-hand way, waving the barrel of his gun towards the living room. The other two men flanking him stepped back to let her pass. Catherine quickly crossed the living room to Mark, who stood to put his arms around her. She buried her face in his neck while he stroked her hair.

"Sit down," said the glasses as, with a practised gesture, he emptied his weapon of used cartridges and replaced them with new. Catherine and Mark sat on the couch, close, but not touching.

"Now please listen carefully. We do not want anyone to be hurt. The dogs startled us, and you can see what happened." He spoke so quietly I had to strain to hear his words. "It perhaps won't surprise you to learn the police are after us. We need a place to hide out for a few hours. We will need a car; we don't know which one yet." Turning to the man on his left, at least six feet six inches tall and emaciated to the point of anorexia, he held a whispered consultation.

"Would all of you please give me your car keys?" he asked with such civility he might be asking the time.

"The keys to the station-wagon are in the brass bowl in the front hall," said Catherine. "I would like . . ." her voice faltered briefly, as she fought back tears . . . "I would like to move the dogs out of the house."

"Jean-Guy will take them outside," he continued, indicating the human flagpole. Then he nodded to the man on his left, small, swarthy, and dressed in the studded leather regalia of a punk fairy. "This is Mikos." On his back he wore a nylon pack-sack, of the sort worn by students to carry books. "And I'm Leslie. Now please give us your car keys."

Larry stood to fish around in the pocket of his jeans. "Aren't you going to rip the telephones out of the wall?"

"You've been seeing too many movies," replied the glasses as he took Larry's keys. I could see Larry giving the leather-clad punk the once-over, that frankly sexual appraisal which begins with the face, moves slowly down to the feet, then zeroes in on the crotch.

From where he stood in the doorway of the living room the

man calling himself Leslie could see the small square telephone table in the front hall, tucked into an alcove formed by the coat closet. "I see you have an answering tape. Will you turn it on, please?"

Mark stood and crossed the room. As he drew abreast of me, he caught sight of the dogs. His jaw went tight. Going into the front hall he switched on the answering machine and returned to sit beside Catherine. "My keys are in the ignition," he said.

The tall man addressed as Jean-Guy went into the hall. Seizing one then the other sheepdog by a hind leg, he dragged their bodies through the front door and out of our immediate line of vision.

"My keys are on the dresser in my bedroom," I said. "Shall I get them?"

"Mikos will follow you." I walked down the hallway to my room, Mikos behind me. By now he had removed the packsack and placed it on the floor, just inside the living room door. I cannot say I relished the situation, novel though it may have been, of feeling a gun pointed at my back. He stood at the door of my room as I picked up the keys.

He gestured with his hand to indicate I was to precede him back to the living room. As I handed the keys to Leslie, he thanked me. It is odd how concealing the eyes robs the face of identity. I would have pegged him as being in his late twenties, as the other two probably were. His light-brown hair had been cut short, but by a good barber. His nose was straight, mouth wide, skin clear. But as I looked at where his eyes should be I saw only my own face, bent and distorted as in a fun-house mirror.

"What is your name, ma'am?" Leslie asked, turning to Catherine.

"Mrs. Bradford."

"Mrs. Bradford, would you please make us something to eat. Mikos will go with you to the kitchen."

Wordlessly Catherine stood and walked across the room and down the hall. As Mikos turned to follow I could see he had three gold studs in his left earlobe.

Leslie handed the sets of car keys to Jean-Guy, who went outside, no doubt to decide which of the cars to steal. No sooner had he left than Mr. Bradford came down the staircase and into the living room. He had changed his shirt and knotted an ascot inside the collar, which made him look dapper in a dated way. Apparently not noticing the gun Leslie held in his right hand, Mr. Bradford assumed these were guests, and nodded politely. "How do you do. I'm Roger Bradford, Catherine's father. I must have dozed off. I could have sworn I heard shots, but it must have been a dream."

"It's not dream," replied Mark. "Come and sit down. We are being held hostage by the bank robbers, this man and his two associates. They held up the bank in town yesterday. Right?"

Leslie gave an affirmative nod.

"They are armed," Mark continued, "and they just shot the dogs. They are not fooling around."

"They did what!" Mr. Bradford's question came out as an exclamation.

"They shot the dogs," repeated Mark patiently. "Now please come and sit down."

Mr. Bradford shook off his son-in-law's restraining hand.

"You mean to tell me these men forced their way into this house and that those shots I thought I heard were real shots?" He took a threatening step towards Leslie, who took one step backward and aimed his gun at Mr. Bradford's chest.

"Do as the man says, and go sit down." He made a threatening gesture with the Magnum which Mr. Bradford chose to
ignore.

"I will not be ordered around in my daughter's house by the
likes of you."

I decided it was time to intervene. "With due respect, Mr.
Bradford, please do as this man says and take a seat." Obviously
my opinion carried more weight than Mark's for I could see the
older man hesitate and consider. But he steadfastly refused to
sit down. How to convince him to put his buns into a chair was
going to take more cajoling and psychology than I was capable
of mustering at the moment.

Larry came to the rescue. "Come on, Mr. Bradford. Sit down
and take a load off your arch supports."

Mr. Bradford turned towards Larry. "I'll have you know I
never wear arch supports, not even in my golf shoes." Having
delivered himself of that revelation he sat in one of the armchairs facing the fireplace. Still not totally mollified, he retied
his ascot, tugged at his sleeveless sweater, bulky enough to have
been hand knitted, and smoothed his hair. "Did Robert and
Elizabeth go out for a walk?"

Larry caught my eye. Of all the dumb questions! In an attempt
to distract them from Mr. Bradford's gaffe, Larry stuck his hand
into the air and spoke. "Please, teacher, may I leave the room?"

But Leslie had been paying attention. "Who are Robert and
Elizabeth?" he demanded, a note of menace in his voice.

Everyone looked hard at the floor except Mr. Bradford.
"Robert is my grandson, and a fine young man he is too. Elizabeth is Mr. Chadwick's niece. Charming girl. I knew her mother

years ago."

"They have gone across the lake to a barbecue," I proffered. "They will be gone for most of the afternoon, maybe longer." I couldn't help thinking of my sister Mildred and of how I had failed to keep an eye on her daughter. Not only had she managed to throw a leg over the son of the house, she stood in a fair way to walk right into the middle of a hostage-taking incident.

"A barbecue," repeated Leslie, almost to himself, as he pondered the prospect of two more people who could walk in at any time.

"Yes, a barbecue," repeated Larry. "That's where you take raw hamburger and coat it with cinders."

"Larry . . ." Mark spoke the name once, quietly.

"I find this perfectly *outrageous!*" Mr. Bradford spoke for us all.

We lapsed into silence. Anyone looking through the window might easily have taken us for a group of passengers on a train who have been informed there is yet another delay. Mr. Bradford sat primly, lips pursed, hands folded in his lap. Larry sat with his legs crossed, his left hand tucked under his right thigh. Mark looked stunned, as well he might. I shifted nervously. The dogs had been shot dead. We were being held prisoner by three armed men. Somebody's car was about to be commandeered. At the same time I was wondering if there was anything, anything at all, I might do. Nothing physical or drastic. The sight of those weapons was enough to scare anyone into compliance. But I was the lawyer among us, even though I had not studied criminal law since I left university. Still, I might be able to reason with Leslie, obviously the leader, if only I could manage to speak with him alone. I would have to wait for that opportunity. But in the meantime, the best course of action was to sit tight and do nothing.

As if reading my mind Larry shrugged. "Just think: things could be worse. We could be sitting in a traffic jam on the Autoroute."

"We could at that," I replied.

I don't know how many minutes passed; I had left my watch on the dresser beside my car keys. Time hung suspended as we sat, pointedly not looking at one another, as if each of us felt profoundly embarrassed for being in this unfortunate predicament.

Mikos leaned casually against the door-jamb, having traded places with Leslie who had gone to the kitchen where I could see him speaking with Catherine. Mikos struck me as the kind of man who does everything as if he is being followed by an invisible and admiring camera. Today he was Mikos, dressed in his punk, Mary-macho leather gear, playing bank robber on the lam. He held the gun as if it were a prop, not an extension of his hand.

Jean-Guy came in from outside and went into the kitchen to speak briefly with Leslie, who then came down the hall into the living room.

"Mr. Crosby," he began. "I just spoke with your wife. I am sorry about the dogs. We had no way of telling they wouldn't attack. Many people who live in the country keep guard dogs for protection."

"Does this strike you as the kind of house where pets go for the throat?" asked Larry.

"I wasn't talking to you," snapped Leslie. "We will remain here until after dark. We will have something to eat, then sleep in tandem. You will remain here in this room. We want no trouble. Nothing will happen as long as you remain quiet. Do nothing to alert the other two when they return. Just let them come inside. We will explain the situation. Nothing will happen to them. Please don't try anything foolish. Remember, one of us will have you covered at all times. We will be taking the Oldsmobile. It has the most gas."

"Looks like I've won," said Larry wryly. "Now may I please go to the bathroom?"

Leslie nodded, indicating Mikos was to follow Larry down the hall. As he passed my chair, Larry winked conspiratorially. "Don't worry. I'll turn on the tap. I'm every other inch a lady," he said so only I could hear.

A few moments later the two men reentered the room. "Who's for another bloody Mary?" suggested Larry.

I looked at the ice cubes expiring slowly in the dregs of my drink, then shook my head at Larry. I had an uneasy feeling it was going to be a long afternoon, and I wanted to keep my head straight.

"No takers?" Larry turned and winked at Mikos. "You'd better come and cover me." The remark sounded dirty. Mikos crossed to stand in front of the fireplace from where he could see into the dining room. I could only speculate on how much vodka Larry was pouring into his glass. I suspected a good deal.

As Larry crossed to sit down Leslie spoke. "Do you have any coffee?"

"My wife could make some," answered Mark. "Do you want me to ask her?"

"No, you stay here. I'll go." With a sign indicating Mikos was to cover the room, Leslie went down the hall into the kitchen.

If Larry was only every other inch a lady, Catherine was the real thing. Even under these difficult circumstances, and her pets having just been shot, she was still playing the hostess. In short order, she had heaped a platter with sandwiches. In his free hand Jean-Guy carried paper plates and napkins which he placed on one of the maple slab tables. Catherine offered a choice of milk, tomato juice, or freshly brewed coffee.

It was curious to watch her, quite literally under fire, deal with the protocol of a lunch in the lounge, or the trenches depending on one's point of view.

First she passed the platter to her father, who loftily announced, with a mouth so tight it looked closed by a draw-string, that he would not break bread with criminals. Larry, whom I had watched eating a lumberjack breakfast, giggled and fired off his tired old line about never eating on an empty stomach. Not having eaten any breakfast myself, I took a sand-wich. So did Mark. Mikos handed us each a paper plate and napkin. I wouldn't have been surprised to learn that in an earlier incarnation he had been a waiter.

Finally Catherine passed the sandwiches to Leslie, to Mikos, to Jean-Guy. By now they were seated on straight-backed dining room chairs placed near the door leading into the front hall-way, from where they could survey the front door, the kitchen, and the living room. Had I been wearing a hat I would have taken it off to Catherine. Not only had she observed the social niceties, she had also established the pecking order. Armed or not, the unwelcome intruders must wait their turn.

We ate in silence. The three men were obviously famished and fell upon the food with great ravenous bites. With Mikos padding obediently behind her, Catherine returned to the kitchen to cut more sandwiches.

After cleaning the platter once again and dividing up the remainder of the apple pie Catherine had offered me at three A.M., washing it all down with black coffee, the three men began to relax. Their posture loosened; their movements became less wary. The rest of us sat quietly, even Larry. I had not realized until then how much the presence of firearms can dampen conversation.

Mark rose to his feet. "Leslie, may I have a word with you in private? We can go into the kitchen."

Light bounced off the eyeglasses as he nodded approval. The conference did not take long. Mark preceded Leslie back down the hallway. In a low voice Leslie told the other men they were to cover the room.

"Geoffry," said Mark. "Would you come with us, please?"

Glad of the chance to move, I stood and walked into the hallway. Mark indicated with his hand that we were to go outside. He held the door, which the intruders had locked, open for me, then followed. Leslie opened the door for himself, followed us outside, then stood a few paces away, holding the gun so the barrel pointed at the ground.

Mark spoke quietly. "I asked him if we could bury the dogs so Catherine won't have to see them again." The two bodies lay on the grass to the right of the front door.

"The shovels are in the garage," said Mark so Leslie could hear. We moved slowly away, Leslie following.

I was touched by this expression of Mark's consideration for Catherine. Not that I was surprised. Even though Mark got himself hopelessly tangled up in surface details and role playing, fundamentally he had always been a kind man.

The car driven by the bank robbers sat behind Catherine's station-wagon just beyond the front door. A dark-green Mercedes-Benz, it had probably been stolen. But whether the choice of a prestigious getaway car had been deliberate or not, the sleek Mercedes looked perfectly at home in front of this prosperous house. The building was not visible from the main road, and even an amateur would know enough to change licence plates on a stolen car. There was little or no chance the automobile, even if reported missing, would be spotted.

A side door led into the garage. Mark turned to Leslie. "May I go in and get two shovels?" The glasses nodded. Mark opened the door on whining hinges, went inside, and shortly emerged with two spades.

"I think over there. At the end of the lawn before we get to the trees."

We walked back past the house, each of us carrying our spade. As we drew abreast of the dead dogs Mark reached down and grasped one of the animals by the foreleg. "Caliban," he said softly.

I reached for the other animal, astonished by the weight of the inert body. Mark was visibly shaken. Although not a pet lover myself, I could not be indifferent to the sheer waste, the casual and wanton taking of life. I understood how much these dogs must have become an integral part of the household. Had they been less guileless and trusting they might still be alive.

We dragged the bodies across the lawn to a point where it narrowed, tapering off to a point in a stand of cedar trees.

"Here," said Mark. Placing the tip of his spade on the grass he placed his foot on the top edge and shifted the weight of his body onto that foot. The blade sank into the ground.

"You do the same, about four feet away and parallel to me."

Leslie stood a few yards distant, one foot resting casually on a low dry-stone retaining wall marking the lower edge of the lawn. Such few 5-BX exercises as I do whenever I think of it, which isn't often, had not prepared me for the rigours of digging through solidly rooted grass into a latticework of fine roots from surrounding trees. By the time we had peeled back the turf of an area roughly four by five feet I was beginning to sweat into my daisy fresh, one hundred per cent cotton shirt. Mark worked steadily, positioning his spade, throwing his weight easily onto the blade, giving one forward thrust, one backward to loosen the soil, then lifting it out to pile it neatly to one side.

Soon we had dug deep enough so that it was no longer practical to work from the edge of the trench.

"There's not room for the two of us," suggested Mark. "I'll dig for a bit; you take a break. It's hard work, I know."

"You noticed."

He stepped down into the hole. "I'll owe you for this, Geoffry."

"And I won't forget it. Now dig."

He began to loosen soil as I stood leaning on my spade, grateful for the respite and noticing, not without a twinge of satisfaction, that Mark too had wet patches on his shirt. My little breather was interrupted by the sight of a bright orange Datsun bouncing down the long driveway at a sporting clip. I remembered Robert's car was bright blue, so at least my niece was still at large.

"Looks like we have company," I announced.

Leslie coiled like a rattler. "Quick! Drop those shovels and get back into the house. Move it! Now!"

There was no mistaking the urgency of the order. Mark and

I dropped our spades and moved towards the house. "Run!"
Leslie barked. Mark and I sprinted up to the porch, Leslie following in a commando crunch. The car continued to move
towards the house.

We ducked through the porch door into the living room
and, winded, dropped into our seats.

"Somebody's coming," announced Leslie, quiet, tense.
"Remain perfectly still. Let whoever it is come inside."

The car crunched past the house and skidded to a stop.
Then we heard the car door close. Footsteps on the gravel.
Then a voice singing in a cracked contralto. " 'Here she comes,
Miss America.' Anybody home?"

The front door, which had not been relocked, opened.
Madge, resplendent in a white pant-suit and persimmon blouse,
came into the living room. "I just dropped by to pick up the
evening bag I left accidentally on purpose." Then she caught
sight of the armed men. "Oh! I see you have company: Curley,
Larry, and Moe."

"Sit down." Leslie indicated the second armchair facing the
fireplace beside that occupied by Mr. Bradford. Madge was
cool. She sat, carefully pulling up her trousers both to preserve
the crease and to display the ankles of which she had just cause
to be proud. Digging around in her capacious straw bag she pulled out a silver lamé case and slid out a pair of white butterfly
glasses with rhinestones on the temples. She put them on, then
fished around for a mother-of-pearl compact which she snapped
open for a quick look at her appearance. "Gawd! If I'd know I
was going to be a hostage I'd have spent more time on my face.
I look like the picture of Dorian Gray." Closing the compact
and dropping it into her bag, she rummaged around until she

unearthed a package of Camels. Teasing a cigarette from the soft paper pack and lodging it in the corner of her mouth, she returned to pillage for matches.

"I don't like smoking," said Leslie.

Madge ignored him. Mr. Bradford picked up a book of paper matches from the occasional table separating the two chairs and lit her cigarette. Madge leaned towards him, covering his hand with hers. "Thanks, hon." She inhaled so deeply I would not have been surprised to see smoke coming out of her straw wedgies.

"I said I don't like smoking." Leslie's voice was quiet but ominous.

"That's your problem, not mine." Madge exhaled. I was sure her lung walls must have met in the middle.

By way of reply Leslie crossed the room to where she sat and slapped the cigarette from her right hand with his left. If the blow stung, Madge did not let it show. For a moment their eyes met, locked.

"Pick that up," she said, "before it burns the carpet."

Leslie shifted his weapon from right hand to left. His posture crackled with menace as he stood, tall and threatening, in front of the seated woman. For a moment I thought he might strike her, a belt across the face with the back of his hand.

Suddenly he stooped to pick up the smouldering cigarette which he ground against the stone fireplace before flicking the butt onto cold ashes.

Catherine stood. "Leslie, this is my house. You may be armed, but this is still my house. If Mrs. Harrington wishes to smoke she will smoke. Do you understand?"

Not being able to see his eyes, I had to read Leslie through body language. He stood straight, squared his shoulders, and aimed his glasses at Catherine. "Mrs. Bradford, I realize this is your house, but you will have to understand that I am in charge. At least until we leave. I am allergic to cigarette smoke. No one will smoke while I am here."

"Not to worry, sweetie," Madge waved her hand in a gesture of dismissal, "I've been meaning to give them up for the last fifty years."

"Can I get Mrs. Harrington a drink?" asked Larry.

Leslie nodded permission.

Larry gestured toward me with a courtly flourish. "His Way-Way-Upness, Sir Geoffry of Chadwick, made a batch of bloody Mary mix."

From a seated position Madge bowed in my direction. "Begging your pardon, sir; in sooth I wouldst a bourbon on the rocks."

The statement sounded so droll in her flat-tire voice that I almost laughed. "Milady, no offence meant, none taken; I warrant thee."

"Mikos, you're on." Larry stood and reached for his own empty glass. "It's jut like trying to get into your safety deposit box," he explained to Madge. "Someone at your elbow every second." He went into the dining room.

Mikos crossed to stand in front of the fireplace from where he could watch Larry. He stood, one leg in front of the other, so that his schlong, clearly outlined by the shiny black leather, swelled against the inside of his right thigh. I was reminded of a "party record" I used to hear at gatherings when I was young. A smutty little song about fishing, it ended with the refrain: "The big ones may weigh more on the scales, but the little ones have those great big tails." He was obviously preening himself for Larry's benefit, possibly for mine. Even armed he was available. A cheap trick, with or without firearms, remains a cheap trick.

Larry came back into the living room carrying two glasses. "Thanks," he said to Mikos, giving him a blatantly sexual wink. If Larry ever gets as far as the pearly gates he'll try to put the make on St. Peter. As he handed Marge her bourbon I could see he had given up bloody Mary mix and moved on to vodka on the rocks. I hoped it was only vodka. If it was gin we were in trouble, more trouble, I suppose I should say.

"Larry, if I were doing a crossword puzzle, how many letters would I need to describe the contents of your glass?"

"Three. It's a good number. Beats two any day."

My heart leaped down. Larry was well on his way to getting drunk. His intoxication does not show in obvious, vaudeville ways. He does not lose co-ordination, stumble about, slur his speech. He just becomes erratic, wild, totally unpredictable. Also he grows as randy as a billygoat. He turns contrary and childlike, to the point where if you ask him to sit down he will stand. Should you suggest he slow down drinking he will fill his glass to the top with neat liquor. Larry can be a catalyst in any situation. Considering our present predicament he had me frankly worried.

Madge stirred her drink with her finger, took a sip, made a wry face. "That's mighty strong, for a sweet young thing. I think I'll add a couple of ice cubes," she said to no one in particular as she got to her feet.

"Sit down, ma'am," said Leslie.

"Send your friend to see I don't do anything naughty," replied Madge as she headed towards the dining room.

"I said sit down!"

"And if I don't are you going to shoot me? For getting an ice cube? Add murder to armed robbery and kidnapping? And when they catch you, and they will, you'll end up so far up the river we'll have to send messages by satellite." She continued to the bar, got herself ice, and returned to her chair.

"Just don't try anything," said Leslie. It sounded lame, in spite of the weapon.

"Like what? Run away? How far do you suppose I'd get? I'm an old lady." She sipped her drink. "Ah, that's better. Besides, these people are my friends. You don't walk out on friends who are in a tight spot. At least we don't."

I tried to hide a smile. The three hoods had just been assigned to limbo.

"By the way," Madge continued, "have you worked out some sort of arrangement for bathroom fatigue?"

"Jean-Guy will take you."

Followed warily by Jean-Guy, Madge carried her bag down the hall where we heard her lock herself into the bathroom. Country houses are not as soundproof as city dwellings. The flush was clearly audible. Time passed. Madge did not open the door.

Jean-Guy rapped nervously. "What are you doing in there?" he asked in heavily accented English. I could see him from where I sat.

"I'm having a cigarette." Madge's voice came clearly through the hollow frame door.

"You'd better come out."

"Not until I've finished. Your friend in there doesn't like smoking."

Jean-Guy stood outside the bathroom door, well over six feet of irresolution. Finally the door swung open. "I'm just putting on lipstick. You can watch if you like."

"Go in there." Jean-Guy pointed towards the living room.

"I always say yes to tall men," replied Madge as she joined us. She crossed to sit in her chair beside both Mr. Bradford and her drink.

"Before you sit down," I said to Jean-Guy as I stood, "I'd like to go to the bathroom."

He stood aside to let me pass, then followed. As I peed, I tried not to look at that ridiculous poem hanging on the wall above the toilet. At the moment a stray Kleenex or two at large in the septic tank seemed a minor issue. I flushed, washed my face and hands, then preceded Jean-Guy back down the hall. From force of long habit I double-checked my fly before entering the living room. Reluctantly, I crossed to sit in my chair. I felt stiff and sticky from shovelling. And the novelty of being held hostage was beginning to wear thin. I was also thinking about my niece and hoping she was having a good enough time to stay wherever she was, at least until the present situation resolved itself.

"Let's draw the curtains and hold a séance," suggested Larry, who I could see had already made a big hole in his glass of gin. "Madame Madge, can you scare up spooks? Do you suppose you could put me in contact with my great-uncle Stacey? He buried eight gold bars in his back yard, and no one has ever been able to find them."

Madge hoisted her drink. "By the time I've had another of these I'll be able to put you in contact with anything." She turned toward Leslie. "Are you aware the police have an accurate description of all three of you going out over the radio? How far do you think you'll get?"

"We'll manage," he replied with a shrug. "A different car, new plates, driving at night."

"Is that the payroll in the packsack?"

He shrugged.

"Loot? In a packsack?" She took a long swallow of her drink. "No style. It's got to be carried in a classy briefcase, or a little black bag, like a doctor's."

"We'll try to do better next time," he replied.

"As I was late for the party," continued Madge, "did I miss the scene where you tell all these nice hostages why you went wrong? Have you tried to wring their hearts and enlist their sympathy with a hard-luck story? Sensitive kid who started out wanting to be a violinist. The drunk father who beat up on you; the saintly sap of a mother who scrubbed floors on her hands and knees; the retarded kid brother; and the sister who put out for everyone in the neighbourhood? Seduced by a Jesuit at seven, then expelled from the seminary for pinching religious objects from the chapel and putting them into hock?"

"That wasn't quite the way it went," said Leslie in a controlled tone. He was now seated with the gun resting on his leg. "It was my sister who scrubbed floors and my mother who put out. She used to work St. Catherine Street wearing a white pantsuit with an orange blouse. Ten bucks for twenty minutes. It bought groceries."

Far from being abashed, Madge let out a whoop of laughter. "Honey, she overcharged. Dressed like that she wasn't worth more than five. Now can I go and stand on the porch, where you can see me, and smoke a cigarette?"

"No."

Madge mouthed something soundlessly. To me it looked like

"sonofabitch." During this exchange Mark, along with Catherine and Mr. Bradford, had sat quite still, their expressions totally noncommittal, as though they were passengers on a subway train invaded by a group of Jehovah's Witnesses. Things scrupulously ignored do not exist.

Mark spoke. "May we, Mr. Chadwick and I, go out and finish our job?"

"No, I'm sorry but it will have to wait. We could be seen. We will remain indoors." He shifted the position of the gun resting on his right thigh, only slightly, but enough to remind us who was in charge. Catherine placed her hand on Mark's knee, a simple gesture but an intimate one.

I cleared my throat. "At the risk of sounding like one of those rehabilitated drunks who organize social activities aboard a cheap Caribbean cruise ship, why don't the four of you hold a return engagement at the bridge table? I don't think Leslie would object." I turned to him. "They will be easier to monitor grouped around a table. And it will help to pass the time until dusk."

"I couldn't possibly play under these circumstances." Mr. Bradford spoke from a great distance.

"Come on, Roger," said Madge. "You and I will take on Larry and Catherine. It will take my mind off smoking."

Catherine stood. "May I bring in the bridge table from the dining room?"

Leslie nodded. Catherine carried in the card table, unfolded the legs, and set it down in front of the fireplace. Four dining room chairs were ferried into place, cards and scoring pad retrieved from the chest of drawers in the front hall, and in short order a bridge game was in progress.

"Why don't you go and sit on the couch," Leslie suggested to me. "Then you will all be in my line of vision."

Obediently I crossed the room to sit on the couch beside Mark.

IX

I found it extraordinary to watch how the mystique of bridge absorbed the four players. They might have been any four people anywhere in the world settling down for a Saturday afternoon at the card table. Catherine took charge of the score pad. Mr. Bradford shuffled the cards. His back was towards me, but I could see he had answered the clarion call, the temporary inconvenience and indignity of hostage-dom forgotten. Larry announced to the world at large that he felt lucky, and Madge observed that if he overbid he'd be shot. The two of them then dissolved into a fit of silent laughter shared by no one else. But once the cards had been dealt, hands picked up and arranged in sequence of suits, the game started in earnest. Barely audible beyond the table, the cryptic bidding exchanges began.

Our three captors had resumed their seats by the door leading into the front hall, where they sat, almost primly, like chaperones at an orgy, guns resting in their laps like reticules. Leslie whispered something to Jean-Guy, who rose and went down the hall. After he had used the toilet I could see him go into Larry's bedroom, presumably to catch a brief nap. I imagined they had all been short on sleep since the robbery, a realization wihch did not help calm me down. The combination of fatigue and tension could be explosive, especially when released through firearms.

As a result I was relieved to see Larry and Madge temporarily occupied by the cards. The pressures of the game would slow down their mouths. So far Leslie had dealt with them well; he was obviously no dummy. But there was no telling when one of their little zingers would find the chink in the armour and earn the perpetrator a crack across the temple with a gun barrel. Nobody likes to be thought a coward, certainly no one brought up in that moronic manly tradition of the charge of the Light Brigade and those who froze solid trying to discover the South Pole.

I hated the idea of being ordered around by these punks. But in that dreary condition known as real life an adage prevails: He who has his finger on the trigger calls the tune. I could tell Mark understood the real gravity of the situation; so did Catherine. Mr. Bradford was operating on the premise that only a cad would pull a gun on a lady, and he refused to hob-nob with cads. Larry is such a compulsive confessor, I would certainly have heard about it had he ever been held hostage against his will. With his endless appetite for novelty, I sensed he was enjoying himself hugely. If we got out of this intact, he'd be drinking out on the episode for months.

Madge puzzled me, and at the same time bothered me. She was making Leslie nervous, and to see Leslie nervous made me very, very nervous. Either she did not realize she was courting danger, or she understood and didn't care. I felt certain Madge had see a thing or two in her long life. In earlier times she could easily have been mixed up with the underworld, as people of my parents' generation would have called it. A misnomer if ever there was one. Those who live outside the law must be very much on top of the world if they are to survive. Maybe Madge had been in tight situations before, but her wisecracking, antagonistic attitude was not making our circumstances any easier, or ensuring our safety.

Perhaps for the first time in my entire life I was beginning to realize what rape is all about. Up to now I had never seriously thought about rape; forcing women to have sexual relations against their will has never been a homosexual preoccupation. Now that I had been forced to watch, impotent, while three men violated Catherine's space I grasped how truly nasty it could be. I do not wish to mangle metaphor, but what is a woman's house if not her own, intensely personal space? The phallic implications of a gun do not need to be underlined. Worse, I had been made to feel like a voyeur, the bystander watching a woman attacked and being powerless to help. Getting myself shot or pistol-whipped, in answer to an empty gesture of adolescent heroism, would benefit no one, least of all Catherine, who would be the first to dissuade me.

I had to consider Mark as well. He was Catherine's husband. This house was his home too. The violation extended to him as he sat beside me, within touching distance on the couch. From where I sat I could turn my head left and see Catherine in profile at the card table, right, I looked at Mark in profile as he sat, elbows resting on his knees, tension flowing from him like a current. I could say I formed the apex of the triangle, with all the stale emotional implications. But the image would not work. I did not wish to drive a wedge into their marriage. At that precise moment I wanted to protect them both, to rid their house of the sullying presence of these three intruders who had rubbed my nose in the unpleasantness of forced entry. Even though they may have raised my consciousness of the fact, I did not thank them. And I was not certain what I must do to put an end to this incident.

A murmur of voices at the bridge table announced the first hand had been played. Larry stood. "Can I go to the bar? I'll be back; never fear. I just made my bid and we're ahead."

"Larry," I began against my better judgement. "Maybe you'd better go slow on that stuff." I knew I was trying to slam a swinging door.

"Chadwick, have you ever been in this kind of situation before?"

"No."

"Then stop trying to write the etiquette book, Mr. Manners. You're just sorry because we're not playing Bingo. O-69." At this last his eyes swivelled away from me and landed on Mikos, who smiled a small, enigmatic, Mona Lisa smile.

On the point of reminding Larry how the French girls who fraternized with German soldiers during World War II had their heads shaved, I heard someone call from outside the house, "Anybody home?" The greeting was followed by a thumping on the screen door, the one beside the fireplace which led onto the porch. Leslie and Mikos sprang to their feet, weapons at the ready.

"I say," repeated the voice outside, "anybody home?"

The banging stopped. Before anyone had a chance to reply – how does one, after all, invite a person into the house to be taken hostage? – Leslie crossed to unlatch the door and admit a couple who looked as though they had just been sent over by central casting. He was costumed as Dr. Watson while she was dressed like the vicar's wife about to spend the afternoon in the potting shed. In her right hand she carried an aluminum pie-plate as though it were the Grail. They did not enter the room; they colonized it.

Ever the perfect hostess, Catherine rose from the bridge table. "Harriet, Nigel, I'm afraid you've dropped in at rather an awkward time. We're being held hostage." She made the observation apologetically, as though she were talking about a badly smoking chimney.

"What a bore!" exclaimed the woman addressed as Harriet. "By whom?"

"By the three men who robbed the bank yesterday."

"That was naughty of them," replied Harriet, who appeared to notice the armed men for the first time.

"That's right," said Leslie in his quiet, off-hand way. "Now please sit down and keep still."

"Please don't point that thing at me," said Harriet, looking not at Leslie but through him. I suspected she had made that same request to her husband on occasion in the bedroom.

Nigel sat on the sofa beside Mark and me while Harriet looked about for a spot to set down her pie-plate. The log table in front of the couch was littered with the fallout of our picnic lunch, not to mention a large ceramic bowl filled with beach glass and pebbles. I watched her glance at the mantelpiece, then reconsider. One does not put home baking on the chimney piece.

"Please sit down," said Leslie.

Harriet continued to look around. About the only clear surface in the room was on the matching table near the bow window. She crossed the room and carefully set down the pie.

"I suppose I should have covered it with a bit of Saran Wrap," she said to no one in particular, "but I was afraid it would stick to the meringue." The pie was an ominous chrome yellow dotted with what looked like slightly scroched plaster of Paris.

"Did you hear me?" hissed Leslie.

"My dear fellow, I am not deaf. And I'm not about to sit holding a lemon meringue pie in my lap while you play your silly games." Giving the pie a half-turn she crossed the room with the obvious intention of sitting beside her husband. This meant I had to stand and give her my seat, which I did gladly. The armchair beside the fireplace was far more comfortable than the couch so I took it.

"Harriet and Nigel Walford," began Catherine in what I had now come to recognize as her hostess voice, "you know my father, of course, and Madge Harrington." Heads bobbed appropriately. "I don't think you have met Lawrence Townsend, a friend from Toronto."

Larry half-rose from his chair. "Hello."

"And Geoffry Chadwick a friend from Montreal."

I stood. "How do you do, Harriet, Nigel."

Harriet Walford inclined her head, the Dowager Duchess of Dorkshire opening a country fair. Nigel Walford half-rose and mumbled something like "Dew-do." By now he had removed his narrow brim tweed hat and unbuttoned his tweed shooting jacket with a leather patch on the right shoulder – clothing way too heavy for the day. Even from across the room I could tell the jacket had never been near a dry cleaning establishment. He wore his hair brushed straight back from his forehead. I am always uneasy around men who brush their hair straight back in an attempt to recreate themselves in their own authoritarian image.

"Leslie and Mikos," concluded Catherine, introducing our captors. "Now can I get you anything?"

"We had late brunch," Harriet announced.

"Eggs and kippers," added her husband.

"So we're not in the least bit hungry," she continued as she worked her way free from a cardigan which looked as though it had been dug out of a compost heap. "We decided to go for a bit of an outing."

"In our skiff," footnoted her husband.

"So we decided to row across the lake and drop in. We beached the boat and came up the path. Didn't realize you had company."

"I wouldn't mind a drop of whiskey," declared Nigel. His remarks came out as a series of tiny explosions. His consonants seemed to ride on jets of steam, not breaths of air.

"Sherry for me, if you have it, or vermouth," demanded Harriet in a voice filled with polo ponies and the British Museum.

"May I?" asked Catherine, turning to Leslie. He nodded and stood to watch her as she crossed to the bar in the dining room.

"By the way, Harriet," began Mr. Bradford, "thanks awfully for the pie. How did you know lemon meringue was my absolute favourite?"

"Oh, it's not for you, Roger. It's for Vera Blakelock. Her husband's having a bit of a turn, something to do with his diverticulum. I had planned to stroll down the road and deliver it in person. I hadn't expected to be delayed. Would someone please be good enough to see she gets it?"

"Certainly," replied Mark.

Catherine reentered the room carrying the drinks she had poured. About to resume her place at the bridge table, she paused. "Perhaps we should postpone the game."

"Good heavens! Please don't interrupt anything on our account!" exclaimed Harriet, setting her sherry glass down with deliberation. Her tone of voice belied the statement.

Without appearing to, I studied the Walfords. They both had that ruddy, wrinkled look of those who believe time spent indoors is time wasted. They were the Campbell Soup kids in late middle age. I'd have been willing to bet cash they still thought in terms of the white man's burden, and on their tea table sat a large glossy volume with photographs of the royal wedding. To live in Canada was to exist in perpetual exile, and they daydreamed a collective dream of a bungalow in Dorset or Surrey or Devon, far from the madding crowd but fully equipped with North American mod cons.

Hostage or not, Catherine had too much social instinct to ignore the new arrivals while she played bridge. "Let's continue the game later on," she offered with a quiet firmness that turned the suggestion into a command.

Under the wary eye of Leslie the bridge game broke up. Madge and Mr. Bradford returned to their armchairs. Catherine folded up the bridge table which she leaned against the fireplace. Larry lined up three of the dining room chairs in front of the chimney. The fourth he carried into the dining room in his left hand, Mikos watching. In his right he held his empty tumbler so as not to waste a trip. It took only seconds for him to splash gin over ice cubes and return to the living room.

Leslie spoke. "You two sit over there." Harriet and Nigel did as they were told. The room was really filling up. Leslie and Mikos sat side by side in the doorway. Clockwise around the room sat Madge and Mr. Bradford facing the fireplace in the armchairs. Harriet, Nigel, and Mark filled the couch under the window. Catherine took the armchair beside the fireplace which matched mine, while Larry perched on a straight-backed chair dead centre in front of the chimney. This position thrust him forward into the room and made him look as though he were a notary about to read a will.

Silence as thick as shaving foam settled over the group.

"Are you planning any trips this summer?" volunteered Catherine, feigning an interest I know she did not feel.

"We were thinking of popping out to Vancouver," replied Harriet as she adjusted the triangular blue bandanna tied around her head and knotted at the nape of the neck – a sure sign she hadn't washed her hair for quite some time.

"To visit our daughter," added Nigel in aspirated appoggiatura.

"And the first grandchild!" announced Harriet proudly. "A little girl, and as good as gold, from all reports."

"It's been my experience," observed Madge, "that kids are only as good as gold when income tax returns are filed. For the rest, by the time they're fit to live with they're living with someone else."

Harriet ignored the interruption. "We thought of motoring down the coast as far as San Francisco," she continued. "We've not been; but Nigel's not terribly keen on the idea."

"The whole damn place is full of homos!" snorted Nigel.

I could barely suppress a groan. All we needed in our Jean-Paul Sartre *No Exit* house party was a homophobe. My own protective colouring is pretty good. To have been married in our society is almost like having a blue and yellow Chiquita Banana sticker on your underwear. This is a real banana. But Larry, especially a Larry on the gin, is liable to gallop full tilt at the windmill. I did not have long to wait. He leaned forward and spoke to the Walfords.

"Did you know that San Francisco was probably the first city where a man could go into a bar and come out?"

"What's so extraordinary about that?" asked Harriet, obviously unacquainted with gay lingo.

Undaunted, Larry tried again.

"Did you know there is something in the air in San Francisco that keeps women from getting pregnant?"

"Pray tell," said Harriet.

"Men's legs."

The snigger from Mikos and giggle from Madge sank into the silence like a penny tossed into a pond.

"If you ask me – " Nigel placed his hands squarely on his thighs – "they should all be rounded up and interned."

"Well, nobody asked you," retorted Larry.

"It would seem to me," I spoke past Larry directly to Nigel, "that you are proposing a violent solution for a non-violent situation. Homosexuals do not roam the streets in packs beating up heterosexual couples. They do not stand outside bars and other watering holes jeering at ladies and their escorts. Believe me, if you decide to visit San Francisco you won't be importuned."

"Maybe that's the problem," interrupted Larry. "The streets are full of men, not choirboys."

"Now just a minute!" The colour rose in Nigel's face, turning his skin from pink to puce. "If it weren't for those armed men I'd take you outside."

"That's the best offer I've had today. In fact it's the only offer I've had today." Larry winked broadly at Mikos, who preened.

"Let's play a game," suggested Harriet, obviously used to her husband's outbursts. "We were at the Dobsons' the other night for dinner and we played charades. It was too amusing." She paused for a whinny of merriment. "Jack Dobson ran around the room waving his arms as if they were wings, and Heather said to him, 'Hello, Enza.' " The memory of that hilarious moment brought on another whinny. "Now can you guess what the word was?"

No one volunteered an answer.

"The word was influenza. In flew Enza."

Larry took a deep swallow of his drink. "I'll go and fool around with the television set, pretending to repair it. Geoffry, you go and ring the front doorbell. We'll be Tinker Bell."

"No, no," interrupted Harriet. "With charades you must act out a word, not a name. Who Was That is the game where you act out the names of people, or characters. Tinker Bell was a person."

"She was a fairy," said Larry, looking directly at Nigel.

Nigel was not amused.

"I like Who Was That bettter than charades," said Madge.

"Good," I said. "Larry, why don't you pretend to play hockey. O.K., Madge, what character from *A Midsummer Night's Dream* comes to mind?"

"Puck!"

"Fuck Puck!" exclaimed Larry.

"I think Oberon already did that," suggested Madge. "He was king of the fairies after all."

"Right in the old bottom!" shouted Larry, obviously out to needle Nigel.

"Wrong," I said. "Bottom was the weaver who caught the eye of Titania, the fairy queen."

"It wasn't the last time a labourer got mixed up with a fairy queen," cackled Madge, who was turning into a front runner herself to be crowned queen of the fag hags. And she and Larry were off again, lost in their shared, secret, silent laughter.

I looked at Mr. Bradford to see how he was reacting to all these cheesy puns, but he seemed oblivious to what was going on around him. He had the air of someone in church who is wool-gathering during the sermon. Mark gave Larry a laser look, which he ignored, while Catherine seemed bemused.

Once in a while it is good for me to have a little taste of group dynamics. It makes me realize why I choose to live alone.

"I don't mind your playing games," announced Leslie, so quietly we all had to strain to hear. "But they will be stationary. Nobody is to run around the room waving his arms or playing hockey."

"What a pity!" exclaimed Harriet. "I suppose that means we can't play In The Manner Of."

"O.K.," said Madge, "I'll bite. How do you play In The Manner Of?"

"It's rather fun really," began Harriet, galvanized by the prospect of organizing a roomful of adults into game playing. She was turning out to be the kind of person I would go to considerable lengths to avoid.

"The person who is 'it' has to leave the room," she continued, as though confronted by a hyperactive kindergarten. "While he, or she, is out of the room, he, or she, chooses an adverb: angrily, sadly, broodingly, any adverb at all. In the meantime, we each have to think up a scenario. For instance, you are a woman who has just been informed that her bank account is overdrawn, or your evening clothes have just been ruined by the dry cleaners. We take turns describing our scenario to the person who is 'it', and he, or she, has to act it out in the manner of the chosen adverb. It's frightfully good fun."

"Who wins and who loses?" asked Madge. "I mean who gets the twenty lashes. Those of us who fail to guess the adverb? Or the person who is such a bum actor that he – or she – can't put the idea across?"

"No one really wins or loses." Harriet gave a shrug of impatience. "One plays for the sheer fun of playing."

" 'When the One Great Scorer comes to write against your name, He marks – not that you won or lost – but how you played the game.' " Nigel didn't even have to think before popping that one on us.

"Well," said Madge, "I guess it beats playing Pin the Tail on the Donkey."

"Not if I'm the donkey," said Larry, and the two of them took off again into their private realm of mirth.

I could almost have envied them. They were adapting to the situation far better than anyone else.

"I went to a party once," began Mark. "As we arrived we all had a name scotchtaped to our backs, a name unknown to us. Then we had to go around asking questions to find out who we were. Once we learned our own identity; say a man turned out to be Romeo, then he had to find Juliet who became his dinner partner. It was supposed to break the ice."

"You sure moved with a smart set," I volunteered.

"I discovered I was Abélard, so I went in search of Héloise. She turned out to be my ex-wife with whom I was not on awfully good terms."

"What we really need," continued Harriet, oblivious to everything but her central preoccupation, "is a game we can all play sitting down."

For one brief, panic-stricken moment I thought Catherine might turn out to own a game of Trivial Pursuit, but she said nothing.

"If I may make a suggestion," I said. "I'll bet anything Nigel and Harriet are both good bridge players. Am I right?"

"Why, yes," replied Harriet, gracious as all hell.

"So is Mr. Bradford. Why not get the game going again? The house is well-stocked with books and magazines, so I can amuse myself. Larry, I'm sure Madge is a whiz at gin rummy. You two could play on the occasional table between the armchairs. I'm sure Leslie would have no objection."

Leslie and Mikos stood, covering us warily, as the players regrouped themselves. Larry and Madge took the armchairs facing the fireplace, then cleared the small table of ashtrays, matches, glasses, and an eskimo carving of a retarded seal. In no time they were deep into gin, bourbon, and gin rummy.

With the look of a Christian martyr being prodded towards the famished lions Catherine unfolded the card table one more time and took her place, prepared to undertake Nigel as partner. Having the sofa once again to himself, Mark swung his feet up and closed his eyes.

I put on my glasses and reached at random for a magazine, opening it to a picture of a young couple running hand in hand through surf towards the camera. I do not like beaches. I do not like to run. I do not like having my picture taken. Holding hands, which have been in salt water, is generally sticky and not nearly as romantic as it sounds.

My gaze wandered around the room and landed on Mark again. I could see his shirt was beginning to dry, as was mine. When we had raced across the lawn, driven indoors by the sight of Madge's car on the driveway, I had caught a whiff of his sweat, musky and warm. Now, as I looked across the room at him. I remembered one June afternoon during a heatwave . . . .

Those were the days when having an air conditioner was morally suspect, and only sissies had electric fans. I had a small and totally ineffectual electric fan. But those delicate souls unwilling to leave a temperature-controlled environment will never know the erotic charge of sexual heat during a heat wave. As sweat pours from pores, so do decorum and inhibition.

In most cases the pathetic fallacy is absurd, but the summer solstice that year coincided with a time of stillness in our own relationship. For that brief, charmed period when we entered into a kind of unspoken truce, the petty bickerings and silly wrangles which occupied so much of our time and used up so much of our energy, had been put on hold. Looking back, I suppose I could say it was one of the few times in my life when the borderline between contentment and happiness blurred. In retrospect I can now tell that my radar, usually alert, had been turned off. Something about our relationship had shifted, but caught up as I was in the mellowness of the moment I never thought to question why or how. All I could think at the time was that somehow we had navigated the choppy straits of learning to accept one another and were ready to drop anchor.

And then one broiling Saturday, a light lunch followed by heavy sex, sex with just the right mixture of lust and laughter, each seasoning the other. Even after three years I still found Mark as sexually dynamic as the day we met. At one point his sweat-soaked body literally slid from my grasp and onto the floor. We laughed in that idiotic way lovers do, for the sheer joy of the laughter itself, then went at one another as though we had just spent six months in solitary.

Lying silently beside Mark, the electric fan whining softly on the dresser, I felt a profound melancholy and thought of

Donne: "Ah cannot we, As well as cocks and lions jocund be,
After such pleasures?" Not normally given to post-coital gloom,
not even during a heat wave, I was suddenly aware of a weight,
a heaviness of spirit. Nor could I find the cause in myself. And
not being one to take the situation lying down, I got up, took
a shower, and suggested we escape the heat by walking up to the
Mount Royal Lookout where there was bound to be a breeze off
the river.

As we walked uphill slowly, steadily, silently, in the hot,
heavy afternoon, I grew aware of the silence between Mark and
me, a quiet so intense as to be tactile. We climbed the concrete
steps from Côte des Neiges and up the steep incline to where the
road levelled out. By now we were both sweating, but the humi-
dity was so intense one dripped standing still.

We continued walking. I have never been given to chatter
for its own sake. Silence can be as companionable and intimate
as a caress. But this absence of words was hedged around with
constraint.

The park teemed with people escaping suffocating rooms
and dressed in a motley array of outfits worn to beat the heat.
Some men had pulled on Bermuda shorts, over black oxfords and
mid-calf socks. A group of women had simply cut the sleeves
out of their shapeless cotton dresses. Another woman wearing
a dressmaker bathingsuit with its short, flared skirt, teetered by
on cork wedgies, her dress over her arm; her companion had
rolled the sleeves of his T-shirt right up to the shoulder. The
eye did not lack for stimulation as we made our way to the
crescent-shaped balustrade commanding a vista of the city,
hazy under a yellow-grey sky.

At the far end of the balustrade, deserted because it faced

into trees, I stopped. "Mark," I began without looking at him, "there's something on your mind. Do you want to tell me what it is?"

"What makes you say that?"

"Ever since we got out of bed the silence has been so dense I could stand on it."

"We don't always have to talk."

"I agree. But there is quiet and there is quiet. One is shared, the other an avoidance. If you don't want to talk about it, fine. But if something is really eating you I would sooner you tell me. Otherwise we'll have a fight, and I'm tired of scrapping."

"O.K., Geoffry. There is something on my mind. And I don't know what to do."

I waited.

"It's us."

"Is something wrong with us? I thought things had been going pretty right for a change."

"They have. It's just that . . . that I'm not certain I want to live the rest of my life as a homosexual."

At that point my radar switched back on. "Do you have any choice? Any more than I do?"

"Yes, I have a choice. Without getting tangled in thickets of philosophy, I believe in free choice. We can all choose the way we want to live."

"And you mean to tell me that you are going to choose a wife and 2.7 children and a white picket-fence and roller skates on the front walk? Come off it, Mark. This is Geoffry Chadwick you are talking to. One who has spent three years with you on the front lines."

"I was afraid you wouldn't take me seriously."

"The problem is I do take you seriously, as seriously as I have ever taken anyone in my life. I love you, Mark." As we had never really been given to verbal endearments that last remark was heavy artillery.

"I love you too, Geoffry." He managed to make the admission seem just a bit shameful, as though he had confessed to having an unpleasant skin disease.

"But you do not want to continue living as one half of a homosexual couple, is that it?"

For the first time he looked directly at me. "Precisely."

At that moment I knew I had lost him. And I was swept with such a suffocating sense of how deeply I did love him I could scarcely breathe, much less answer.

"It is not how I feel about you," he continued. "It's how I feel about myself. I suppose it is cowardly of me, to care about what other people think. But I do care. And I want the kind of life . . . the things marriage can bring."

"Do you have someone in mind?"

"No. The only person on my mind is you. And until –" he faltered – "until you give me up, I won't be able to do anything about anything."

"This is beginning to sound like a scene from Henry James, bad Henry James at that. What you are saying is the decision rests with me: to hang on to you against your will, or to let you go voluntarily."

"Something like that."

"I don't think I am an excessively vain man, Mark; but if I let you go it will be for good. A clean break." In spite of myself I laughed, a short, sharp laugh without mirth. "A break? It will be more like an amputation. Are you absolutely certain about your decision? Do you really want us to separate? Think carefully before you answer. What you decide will profoundly affect both our lives. Do you want me to leave?"

Without speaking he nodded his head up and down, up and down, up . . . For a moment I felt such dizziness I thought I might fall. The feeling passed.

"O.K., Mark. So long then. Take care." I gave a small wave. "See you around."

I turned and walked away. I did not look back. Had I been a character in a movie I would have looked back, for that one, last lingering look that says never is not forever. But I knew he would be weeping. And I did not want him to see my own tears.

X

I must have dozed off in my chair. My head snapped forward and I awoke with a jolt. Almost instinctively I checked my nose to see if my half-spectacles were still in place. They were. As I folded them into their case I thought of how I must look to the others, dozing off in mid-afternoon still wearing my specs. All too soon I would be shuffling along with the aid of a walker. As my watch ticked away on the dresser in my bedroom I had no way of telling how long I had been asleep. Middle-class living rooms seldom come equipped with clocks. Possibly the social strata which is most obsessed with time does not wish to be reminded of that worrying dimension in the room where people "live."

The card games were still in progress. Catherine, who sat facing me at the bridge table, caught my eye. Leaning her cheek against her two hands pressed together she gave me a quick smile, then rolled her eyes to suggest the bridge game was less than jolly fun. Mark still slept on the couch. Madge and Larry played cards like conspirators, heads bent over the table, whispering. From where I sat I could see half-filled tumblers of gin and bourbon under each chair. Jean-Guy, who had now emerged from the bedroom, sat beside Leslie. I presumed Mikos was now taking a brief nap.

My mouth felt like sandpaper. "Catherine," I said, "could I go out to the kitchen and make myself some instant coffee, or tea?"

"I'll get it for you."

No, no. Don't interrupt your game. I'd welcome the chance to move. As Antony said to Cleopatra, 'I am dying of boredom, Egypt.' " I decided to make my move now. "Leslie, would you mind coming with me?"

I stood. So did he, a gesture I took to indicate agreement. I crossed in front of him and we walked down the hall to the kitchen. Since my back was towards him he could not see me smile. As the two of us left the room I could see from the corner of my eye that Madge was already reaching for her bag. At this very second she was probably taking a drag that would burn up one third of the cigarette. I was fearful lest Nigel, who was dummy for this hand, decided he wanted tea as well. Given my choice of being stuck for the afternoon with Nigel and Harriet or three armed robbers, I would be hard put to decide.

On those infrequent occasions when I make tea for myself in my own apartment I just take out a tea bag, toss it into a mug, add boiling water, and yank it out by the string when I can no longer see the bottom of the mug. Hardly your Japanese tea cere-mony; however, I wanted to prolong the break, to postpone returning to the other room as long as possible. Consequently I took down a large brown earthenware pot I had seen last night when I helped Mark to clear up dinner. Tea bags sat in a canister beside the stove.

"Will you have some tea?" I asked Leslie.

"Yes, thank you." He was lounging against the counter at the far side of the table.

I put two mugs and a sugar bowl onto the table. By now the kettle was making reassuring noises, indicating the water had begun to heat up. I turned towards Leslie, folded my arms across my chest, and leaned my butt against the sink. "Why did you rob the bank?"

"Because I wanted the money."

"We hold these truths to be self-evident. Let me put it another way. Do you have a specific purpose for the money?"

"Yes, I'd like to move to British Columbia where the winter is not severe and buy a small business that would allow me to live in the country. What's so funny?"

"Sorry. I know it's rude of me to laugh, especially when I asked the question. But the idea of robbing a bank to finance the bucolic retreat does strike me as bizarre. I mean, do you grab handbags from little old ladies and give the proceeds to UNICEF?"

"I am not a Mickey Mouse hood, not even a Robin Hood. As a matter of fact, I'm not even a professional criminal, at least not until now."

"I can believe that." By now the kettle was becoming very excited. "I don't think a real pro would have gotten himself into this kind of situation with two-thirds of the neighbour-hood held hostage. Why did you pick this house? There must be hundreds around the lake."

"A miscalculation. We thought this house had only an old couple living in it. But having made the error we had to stick with it."

"Whose miscalculation was it?"

"Jean-Guy's"

"It figures. Look, I'm a lawyer. Granted, I'm in corporation law. I haven't really looked at criminal law since I graduated from law school. But I do know that if you are caught you could go to prison for quite some time. Were you to surrender your-selves voluntarily . . ."

"Stop right there. Save your breath to cool your tea."

The water had by now come to a full boil. I scalded the pot, rotating the hot water until the outside felt warm to the touch. Then I dropped in two tea bags, filled the pot with boiling water, and set it on a brass trivet in the middle of the table to steep. Pulling out one of the kitchen chairs I sat. Across the table from me Leslie followed suit.

"Before you cut me off at the knees," I continued, "just consider what I am saying. Remember, I have nothing personal to win or lose, except perhaps an afternoon. Moreover, were I to become in any way involved in this case it would cost me time, my own time. I would be far wiser to shut up and let you leave as planned, after dark. But so far nobody has been hurt, not even seriously inconvenienced. Shooting the dogs was unfortunate; they were not in the least vicious. But under the circumstances it was an understandable mistake, as I would be quite willing to attest. And were you to offer to replace them it would be a point scored. You would never have to, but the gesture would make you seem suitably contrite. Never lose sight of the fact that if you ever do go west, young man, you will walk through your apple orchards or rows of seedling firs a wanted man. You will live in perpetual risk of discovery. Is it worth it? Does the end really justify the means?"

"You left out the bit about my old mother wondering when she will hear from me as she does laundry on a washboard in a galvanized iron tub."

I laughed out loud. "As a matter of fact I had her working as a babysitter by the day, looking after other people's kids. That's far worse than taking in laundry."

Leslie smiled for the first time. His smile was just a little

lopsided. A slight gap between his two front teeth gave to his
expression that slight imperfection which can be more attractive than perfect regularity. At the same time he reached up
and removed his mirrored glasses with his left hand. Placing
them on the table he rubbed his eyes before looking directly at
me. Large, clear, green, his eyes hit me with an almost visceral
impact. To see him without the disguise of the mirrored glasses
made me realize why he was in charge of the operation. More
than merely intelligent or articulate, he had a magnetism that
set him instantly apart from the crowd. Nowadays anyone who
runs for dogcatcher is described in the press release as
charismatic. But whatever it is, Leslie had it. Some people live
in black and white, some in sepia. Then there are those who
move in technicolour.

"Yes," he replied thoughtfuly, "in answer to your question,
the end does justify the means. There is no way in today's
economic situation that I could ever get together enough
money to make a fresh start, not legally, that is. I understand
what I have done, and I am fully aware of the possible consequences. So spare me any observations you might be about to
make on right and wrong. Not all people who behave dishon-
estly are fools."

"You get no argument from me. I have always suspected it
takes not only intelligence but a forceful imagination to be a
successful criminal." I paused to pour tea into mugs, deliberately chosen to keep the tea hot. "Notice how I use the word
successful. The overcrowded state of our jails suggests, to me at
least, that the success rate is not always one hundred per cent.
There's milk in the refrigerator if you want it."

"No, thanks."

"But even in illegal situations," I continued, "there are still responsibilities. What about the two men you have persuaded or hustled or conned into helping you? How did you get them to join in the caper?"

"What makes you so certain it was my idea?"

"That's easy. You are smarter, better educated, more articulate. You have the imagination. You are a natural leader. Without someone like you they would always be small-time hoods, stealing coins from parking meters, pinching handbags from shopping carts in supermarkets."

"Maybe. Jean-Guy's from the Gaspé, north shore. Zero opportunity. He came to Montreal hoping to make it big as a basketball player. He didn't. Mikos wanted to get off the street. He's been a busboy, a short-order chef. He's parked cars and washed windows. An honest day's work doesn't pull in very much these days."

"And having a few thousand dollars in stolen cash will change their lives for the better?"

"Probably not. But I needed them for the job."

"Did they have previous records?"

"No."

"So you used your superior intelligence and powers of persuasion to convince them that your scheme was the best thing for them."

"I guess." He reached for his glasses, which he put back on.

"I wonder if perhaps that isn't more reprehensible than robbing the bank. You have altered the course of their lives, and not for the better. I don't know how much honour there is among thieves, but I think you have more to answer for than just stealing cash. For their sakes, poor dumb clucks that they are, you could think of giving yourselves up, the money intact. I will go to bat for you."

Leslie stood. "Mr. Chadwick, I appreciate what you are trying to do. You're the only person in that room who has any brains. But you're wasting your time. I did not undertake this robbery lightly. And I'm not about to give it all up. Now, if you will be good enough to return to the living room with your tea, I am going to sleep for half an hour."

He held out his hand, the one not holding the Magnum, in a gesture which reminded me of a grade school teacher urging pupils back into school after recess.

"Just a minute more," I requested, "since you are obviously going to carry your plan through to its conclusion, may I ask what you really intend to do?"

"That's easy. We are going to leave. Head for a big city. Disperse."

"What about the borrowed car? Will you leave it where it can be found?"

"Why not?"

"Here, take one of my business cards. When you have abandoned the car, call collect from a phone booth. My secretary can take the message."

He reached for the small cardboard rectangle and tucked it into his shirt pocket.

"What will happen to us?" I continued. "To me? I have seen you without your glasses. Aren't you afraid one of us will finger you?"

He paused briefly before answering. "Not really. By the time you have given a description to the police we will have changed our appearances. After a while you'll shrug the whole thing off as an annoying interruption. You'll think about following it up, but you won't. That is why we are being so careful no one gets hurt. Now, if you'd please go back inside."

I rose and moved around the table towards the hall. I had failed to persuade him to surrender himself to the police, but then at best it had been a long shot. I suppose I really never expected he would, but at least it was worth a try. On the other hand, he had led me to believe there would be no reprisals when they left. I wanted to believe that, very badly. Yet whether or not I could take Leslie at his word, the fact remained that he had a lethal weapon trained on me.

We returned to the living room and Leslie whispered to Jean-Guy, then went down the hall to Larry's room. Shortly Mikos came into the room and took his position beside Jean-Guy.

"Gin! And I think that means game!" exclaimed Madge, laying down her cards with a flourish.

"You stacked the deck," giggled Larry, reaching for his drink.

While Madge was picking up the cards from the gin rummy game there was a flurry of movement at the bridge table.

"That's our rubber," announced Mr. Bradford. "Well done, Harriet."

"I've never been dealt such unfortunate cards," exploded Nigel. I could tell he was the kind of player who was never beaten; he lost only because circumstances were against him.

"Mr. Chadwick, I don't suppose there is a drop of tea left in the pot you just brewed," demanded Harriet, framing the order as a question.

Before I could answer Catherine stood. "I'll go and make fresh," she said. "Mikos, if you please."

When I was a small boy I sat through a great many drawing room comedies. Not by choice I hasten to add. My mother knew some women who were involved in amateur theatre. Knowing my mother was constitutionally incapable of saying no, they would call her when they needed a prop – a chesterfield, a dressing table, two matching chairs. In return for the favour she invariably received two complimentary tickets to the performance. My father was adamant about not attending amateur productions, insisting the audience should be restricted only to blood relatives of the players, and possibly in-laws by marriage. Since Mother did not even like to cross the street alone she dragged me along to those dreadful drawing room comedies, or else Ibsen. Whenever an amateur group wants to be serious, they perform Ibsen. I am convinced the reason I have never spent tourist dollars in Scandinavian countries is a result of my early exposure to all those gloomy Norwegians who shot themselves, turned bonkers from syphilis, drowned in millstreams, fell from steeples, poisoned the water supply.

Most amateur groups, however, loved to play drawing room comedy, the dramatic genre which demands the most deft professional touch to be even remotely plausible. Once the curtain, at least twenty minutes late, had been tugged open to reveal the set, Mother's furniture placed downstage from a pair of French doors opening into a void, then the play would begin. An actress costumed as a maid would be summoned onstage by the telephone, which often did not even ring. If the actress playing the maid could fudge a foreign accent, by definition amusing, so much the better. In short order, she was followed by other actors who believed that if you were playing comedy you must never be still. They jiggled and mugged, jumped cues

and telegraphed laughs as if they were all on Benzedrine. I
failed to find their predicaments amusing. A truthful word, a
yes instead of a no, sometimes a simple boot in the ass would
have resolved a situation which took these inept actors three
whole acts to unravel. My present predicament was not unlike
that of being trapped in a theatre; only there was no way of
leaving before the end of the performance.

Had Ibsen ever taken it upon himself to write a drawing
room comedy I think he might well have hit on something like
a scene where the actors drink tea under the supervision of armed
men. Catherine herself could have written the book on how to
behave with grace under pressure. Carrying a large wooden
tray, she entered the living room, followed by Mikos. Setting
the tray on the card table, the players having resumed their
original places, she went through the ritual hierarchy, giving
priority to age and sex. Madge refused tea, saying she would just
suck away on her bourbon. Harriet asked for her tea with lemon
and a little sugar.

"I see you use the reconstituted lemon juice," she observed,
disapproval dripping from every syllable.

"It's more convenient." Catherine screwed the cap back onto
the small green bottle. I was glad to hear no note of apology in
her voice.

Not surprisingly, Larry refused tea. Mark reached for a cup. I
still had a half-full mug.

Catherine turned to our captors. "Mikos?"

He nodded.

"Milk and sugar?"

Again he nodded. I had yet to hear him utter a word. His
silence was almost as creepy as Leslie's glasses, not to mention

Jean-Guy's elongated emaciation. He looked in profile as though
he had just spent six harrowing weeks on a hunger strike.
Catherine asked him if he wanted tea.

"*Merci.* No, thank you."

I watched with amusement as Mikos rested his pistol on his
knees, pressed together in ladylike fashion. To complete the
image, he crooked his little finger as he drank. He was also
smiling, which surprised me. Men wearing leather never seem
to smile.

As I observed the scene it began to take on the aspect of a
performance. When people spoke I heard the conversation as if
it consisted of memorized lines.

SCENE: *Affluent country living room. Upstage centre is dominated
by a fieldstone fireplace, not French doors.*

CATHERINE: I don't have much to offer in the way of cake or
cookies. Would anyone care for a slightly stale Peek
Frean assortment?

HARRIET: Peek Frean? I think I will.

GEOFFRY: How about a slice of lemon meringue pie?

HARRIET: (*bridling*) Indeed not! That pie is for the Blakelocks.

GEOFFRY: Sorry, I guess I lost my head.

HARRIET: Don't fuss with a biscuit dish, Catherine. Just bring
the tin.

(*Exit Catherine stage left followed by Mikos.*)

LARRY: (*burying his face in his hands, speaking with a mock-
Russian accent*) How much I would like to go to Montreal, for my name day.

MADGE: I can still remember the first time I came to Montreal. We were driving down St. Catherine Street in a limo when the old buck I was with told me it was the main drag. I couldn't believe him. It's the skinniest main drag I ever saw. (*She takes out a cigarette and lights it.*) I've got to catch up on these things before no-eyes gets back.

(*Catherine enters stage left followed by Mikos. She carries a biscuit box.*)

HARRIET: (*reaching for tin*) I always buy Huntley Palmers myself.

CATHERINE: Is that right?

NIGEL: Beggars can't be choosers. (*Laughs. A crypto-military snort.*)

HARRIET: Quite so. (*Looks into biscuit tin.*) Eeny, meeny, miney, moe.

NIGEL: Catch a –

HARRIET: Nigel!

LARRY: That jingle is racist, chauvinistic, and fetishistic. (*He drinks.*)

(*Pause.*)

HARRIET: (*clearing throat*) Do we have any arrangement for the little girls' room?

MADGE: One of the boys takes you down the hall and stands outside the door. You have to run the tap or sing "Rule Brittania" at the top of your voice. It's a man's world, all right. They can aim for the side of the bowl.

LARRY: Really, Margaret!

MADGE: Oh, Lawrence, don't be such an old stick.

(Madge and Larry laugh silently. Harriet rises, crosses to stage left, exits followed by Mikos.)

NIGEL: If you're all tired of playing bridge I know an excellent game. You take a large sheet of paper. I start by writing a phrase or a sentence, then fold the paper so the other players can't see what I have written. I pass the page to the next player and he writes another phrase or sentence . . .

MADGE: He or she . . .

NIGEL: Quite right. After he – or she – has folded the page it is passed on to the next player, and so forth around the room. The last player unfolds the paper and reads the sentences in sequence.

GEOFFRY: And we all roll around on the floor laughing at gibberish?

MADGE: Who wins?

NIGEL: Nobody wins. We play for the sheer amusement.

MADGE: I'm from Missouri. What's the point of playing a game if nobody wins?

HARRIET: *(enters from stage left, followed by Mikos)*I don't think I've ever seen so many Estée Lauder products outside a department store.

LARRY: I used to use Helena Rubenstein, but it's become hard to find. And I prefer the Lauder moisturizer.

NIGEL: But – those products are for women!

LARRY: Men have dry skin too. Would you be happier if I used chicken fat?

NIGEL: Sounds queer to me.

LARRY: The word is gay. Queer is what you are before you know you are gay, zipperhead.

NIGEL: You go too far, my good man.

LARRY: Maybe a good man is what you really need.

NIGEL: Believe me, you haven't heard the last of this.

LARRY: Did you hear what the gay astronomer said to his friend? 'I saw Uranus last night.' And you can kiss mine.

GEOFFRY: Children, children, I realize Christmas is a full seven months away, but let us still try to be good. (*He puts on a stern expression. He is thinking that were this a real play in a true theatre not only would he walk out of the performance but he would go straight to the manager and demand his money back.*)

MARK: (*conciliatory*) I know a card game we can all play. It's called Bump.

LARRY: I like it already.

MARK: It's a variant on poker and it's a game of elimination. No betting. The players all buy three chips for an agreed amount, say a dollar. The dealer deals each player a poker hand and he also deals an extra hand into the centre of the table. If he does not like his hand he can pick up the one in the centre. At the same time he exposes his original hand. The other players can each take a card in turn to improve their own hands. If he decides to keep his hand the next player has a crack at it, and so on. When a player thinks he can beat the weakest hand he says "Bump!" and knocks the table. The other players have one last turn before showdown. Low hand on the table forfeits a chip. You don't have to win, as such. All you

> have to do is beat the low hand. Last person out wins the pot.

MADGE: Sounds as though you have time to draw to an inside straight.

NIGEL: Helena Rubenstein!

HARRIET: Oh, do shut up, Nigel. What damn business is it of yours what Mr. Townsend puts on his face?

(They glare at one another.)

GEOFFRY: Mark, I have three questions. Can you pick up the five exposed cards at one time, the entire hand to re-place with your own? In the case of a tie, say two different pairs of jacks, does high card beat the other out? Can the person who says "Bump" also take a card?

MARK: Yes, yes, and no. Let me also add that you can bump at any time without taking a card, and if nobody takes the hand in the centre the players all show their cards. Low hand loses.

HARRIET: We don't play poker.

MADGE: I thought the U.K. was supposed to be civilized.

NIGEL: It is. And Englishmen do not wear cosmetics.

LARRY: What about the Cold Cream Guards?

NIGEL: I'll have you know my nephew is a guardsman!

LARRY: *Sed quis custodiet ipsos custodes?*

NIGEL: I beg your pardon.

LARRY: 'But who would guard the guards themselves?' That's Juvenal, kiddo.

GEOFFRY: Larry, you surprise me. Who would have thought you would be quoting snippets of Latin?

LARRY: Just because I haven't read a book since I left university doesn't mean I never read one while I was there. I have "Small Latin and less Greek." Or, as the young man said after he was gang raped in jail, "It was Greek to me." *Julius Caesar*. Act I. The character who spoke the line is called Ibid.

HARRIET: Really, Mr. Townsend. Have you no respect for anything, not even our Shakespeare?

LARRY: Shakespeare is all right. It's Dickens who really makes me want to barf. I'm not exactly Casanova, but Dickens really hated women. Look at David Copperfield and those nerds he married. I'll bet he is the only twice-married man in all of literature who has warts on his palm. But I do like Conan Doyle. I think I've read all the Holmes stories. I guess you could call me a Holmophile.

CATHERINE: (*speaking in her hostess voice*) If we're all going to play cards together I suggest we move into the dining room where the table can accomodate us all.

LESLIE: (*appears suddenly in doorway stage left*) Nobody is to leave this room. Put out that cigarette. (*Madge reaches for ashtray. Crossing in front of Mr. Bradford, Leslie takes the half-empty package of cigarettes from the small table, shreds the remaining cigarettes, tears up the package, throws everything into the fireplace.*) We'll be leaving as soon as it's dark. Mrs. Bradford, will you please make us some sandwiches to take along. You will be coming with us, so you may want to pack a small case.

CATHERINE: I beg your pardon?

LESLIE: I said you will be coming with us, as far as Toronto.

Bring a credit card or some cash so you can get back
home. If the rest of you value Mrs. Bradford's safety I
urge you not to alert the police after we have left.

(General consternation.)

CURTAIN

XI

In a second, the scene had shifted. Up to this moment we were a group of wildly mismatched adults forced by circumstances into an intimacy we would never voluntarily have sought. But as the realization took hold that Catherine was to be abducted, I could feel the bond between us tighten as we faced the first real threat to our group. The shared experience of being held captive had turned us unwittingly into members of the same fraternity, and the difference between breaking up voluntarily and being pulled apart made us each, in his – or her – own way attempt to forestall Catherine's forced departure and guarantee her safety.

So much for my pitch in the kitchen, and Leslie's assurance that they were going to leave without making trouble. I was both alarmed and angry that Catherine was to be taken away, out of her own house. She would be in danger. We would be forced to keep the peace. I knew I had to do something, but at the moment I was stumped. Nor could I think of anything reassuring to say that would allay the fear I knew she must be feeling.

Not surprisingly, Larry was the first to speak, breaking the stunned silence which followed Leslie's announcement. "Why don't you take me along instead of Mrs. Bradford. You're taking my car. I have to get back to Toronto anyway. And," he paused for a swallow of his drink, "I'm far more of a lady than she could ever hope to be."

"Well done," muttered Nigel, who only moments earlier would have turned purple at Larry's last statement.

Leslie shook his head. "Sorry, but you're too unpredictable. You might try to pull something, and we'd have to deal harshly with you. And we have our reputations to consider."

Larry looked straight at Leslie. "Know something? I'll bet you're just like Chinese food: happy when you're eaten out."

Catherine was still standing beside the card table where she had been pouring tea. Mark rose from the couch and crossed to stand in front of his wife, so that in effect his body shielded hers. "Please take me along instead. Leave my wife here. I won't give you any trouble." He paused, as if searching for the right combination of words with which to plead his cause. As he stood there tall, honourable, vulnerable, governed by a now outdated code of chivalry, almost boyish in his eagerness to shield Catherine, I found myself affected and all the more determined to find a solution.

Before Leslie could reply, Mr. Bradford pushed his way to his feet. "Catherine is my daughter. If anyone is to replace her it should be me."

"Sorry, sir, but you are too old. If anything should happen to you on the way we could not stop and make sure you got proper medical attention. We could be blamed."

It struck me that much of Leslie's menace stemmed from his unfailing politeness. Had he been loud, or abrupt, even coarse, he would have been almost easier to accept than the soft spoken, courteous man who carried a weapon which could blow a side out of the house.

Catherine moved to stand in front of Mark. With an unself-conscious gesture, she pushed her hair back from her face and turned on Leslie. "You sonofabitch!" Instantly the room snapped alert. "You force your way into my house, shoot my dogs, bully my friends. And now you say I am to drive with you to Toronto? Well, you poisonous little creep, you are going to have to drag me out of here!"

"If necessary we will, Mrs. Bradford."

"And furthermore you can make your own goddamn sand-wiches, unless you want them filled with ground glass."

Although I certainly could not blame Catherine for her outburst I knew it would serve no purpose other than to antag-onize a determined, and I suspected, desperate armed man.

"Catherine," I spoke softly. "I think perhaps you should do as he says. And I think that all of you should sit down." I spoke firmly, and without making the movement too abrupt, stood. The physical gesture of my standing obliged the others to sit, as though I were in control of the seesaw.

Madge spoke. "What you really need for a long drive to Toronto is an old broad who has seen it all and can tell you about it. I'm far more fun than those artsy-fartsy CBC programs you'll pick up on your car radio."

"I'm quite prepared to believe that, ma'am," replied Leslie. "But we don't want to be obliged to stop every fifty miles so you can smoke, or else watch you go into nicotine withdrawal shock." He turned to address the room at large. "Let me assure you all that nothing will happen to Mrs. Bradford outside of being in-convenienced. We are not trying to get ourselves into the tabloids, but safely out of the province and into a large urban centre where we can disappear. Mrs. Bradford will be nothing more than a passenger in the car, and our safe conduct."

During this announcement I had remained standing. "Leslie,

a word with you please in the kitchen." Without waiting for a signal of consent I moved in front of him and strode down the hallway. He had little choice but to follow.

I crossed to sit in the chair directly in front of the kitchen sink. I would have preferred to stand, but my superior height would have turned me into the dominant figure, in spite of his being armed. And I hoped to plead with him through reason rather than intimidation not to take Catherine away.

I gestured to the chair on the other side of the table and he sat down.

"I don't suppose," he said, beating me to the draw, "that you are about to put the arm on me by appealing to my good judgement and better instincts. That we are resorting to barefaced kidnapping. That if we are caught they'll throw the book at us. That a true gentleman would not drag a wife from her home and husband. And finally, you probably have a son about my age, and you would hate to think of him screwing up his life just as I am about to screw up mine?"

I thought quickly. Of course he had hit the nail squarely on the thumb, and it smarted. I had entertained every intention of arguing along the lines he had suggested, in effect trying to appeal to his intelligence and code of ethics. That he had intelligence, I could not doubt. That he had a code of ethics, I did doubt, or that it certainly was different from mine.

"What do you take me for? I may be a liberal, but my heart does not bleed. I have an alternate plan, which, if you will hear me out, will be the better for everyone concerned. I am operating on the principle that the best way to hide something is not to conceal but to camouflage. A friend of mine once had her house burgled. She had taken the precaution of keeping her good jewellery in a shoe box full of junk jewellery she kept for her granddaughter to play with. The thief dumped the box, saw the junk jewellery, and left it all to search for more valuable items. The truly valuable items were overlooked. O.K.?"

Leslie nodded.

"By the same token the police will expect you to head for Montreal. And through their network of informers, stoolies – don't we all watch *Hill Street Blues?* – they will hope to get a lead on you somewhere, somehow. And they might, if you hide out downtown, in the north end of the city, or the east end. But not even the most astute detective would expect you to conceal yourselves in Westmount."

"Could be."

I leaned forward and dropped my voice, the oldest trick in the business for making a point. "I live in an apartment smack in the middle of beautiful downtown Westmount. I have a parking spot in the garage, which is in the basement and from which I have access to the elevator. We take my car, I drive to Montreal, park as usual in my parking space; then the four of us ride the elevator up to my apartment where you will be as well hidden as you could be anywhere in the world. It will mean a couple of days of take-out food, chicken, pizza, Chinese; but there are worse things to eat."

"But your friends in there. They will know where we are."

"Not if you tell them we are driving straight through to Toronto. You can count on my silence. If I blurt out the truth then my plan goes out the window."

"The Autoroute will be watched."

"We will take the old road, now a secondary road. I suggest you put Jean-Guy in the front seat with me while you and Mikos hunch down in the back seat. We will look like two passengers out for a Sunday drive on the holiday weekend."

"What about licence plates on your car? Your friends will surely report them. The police could spot the numbers."

"Easy. Go and cover up the plates on my car until we have left. Even better, switch plates with one of the other cars."

"But your friends will still alert the police to look for a medium-grey Cadillac."

On the Autoroute, four passengers. We will be two passengers dawdling along secondary roads."

Leslie sat, obviously weighing my plan. Thoughtfully he removed his glasses.

"You live alone?"

"Yes."

"Divorced?"

"No."

"Are you gay?" His green eyes trapped mine.

"Let us just say I am not unacquainted with that particular lifestyle. Are you?"

"When it is convenient."

We were still looking at one another, hard. It has often been said that a look can speak volumes; but this eyelock was more like a telegram, clear, condensed, its message intensely sexual.

"And when it's not?"

"Then I please myself."

"Is that how you enlisted Mikos?"

By way of reply he gave a shrug. "I guess he's pretty easy to spot."

For a moment his faced relaxed into a smile. Then he drummed the fingers of his left hand nervously on the table. "What if we are seen entering your apartment? Do you have a doorman?"

"Yes, but we're unlikely to meet him. He stays in the lobby. At any rate, even if he did see you, he would just assume I was with some friends. The only ones who might see us on the elevator are other residents. And they all make a habit of looking at the floor if anyone else is in the elevator."

He continued to tap the fingers of his left hand nervously on the table.

"Think of it this way," I continued. "You will have kidnapped a man, a single man at that, a transient guest in the house. That alone will cause far less indignation than taking a married woman from her own home. It's a crime, sure; but were you ever caught it would sit far more easily with a jury. Think about it, carefully."

Suddenly Leslie reached for his glasses, and using one hand hooked the temples around his ears.

"No dice, Mr. Chadwick. First of all, I don't know your setup. I don't think you are leading us into a trap, but . . ." he paused, "you are intelligent. And that's what scares me about you. You're too plausible. If you've given me second thoughts, God only knows how you would work on those two wimps in there. What happens if you persuade them that their interest is not my interest? It's two against one. I would have to monitor you every second. And locked up with you for forty-eight hours or more? Nothing doing. It's too risky."

"I'm not about to get myself shot, nor my apartment trashed."

"I know that. And we are three versus one. But you're too damned clever, not to mention being a lawyer. I can't afford to take the chance."

"You can't afford not to!"

"I'm not changing my mind."

"In that case let me say only this. Obviously you cannot be reached by reason, so I shall have to resort to threat. Even though you are carrying a gun, I am giving you a warning. If you take Mrs. Bradford out of this house I shall do everything I can to have you brought to justice. Up to now I have not been unsympathetic, but I will personally offer a reward for information leading to your arrest. I will do this, believe me, so I entreat you for the last time: do not take Catherine Bradford away."

Leslie stood. "I think we had better get back to the living room." He made a motion with his gun that left no doubt I was to move.

I had struck out again. Persuasion had failed. A threat had also failed, although bluster, even controlled bluster, is nothing against a bullet. Short of getting myself shot I could see no solution other than seeing Catherine go and hoping she would emerge intact. Well, maybe some sort of opportunity would present itself, although I did not feel very optimistic as I left the kitchen.

We rejoined a sober group. Even Larry and Madge had fallen uncharacteristically quiet. I knew Madge was gamely trying not to think of her cigarettes now scattered across the layer of wood ash in the fireplace. Nigel Walford had switched places with Catherine, who sat beside Mark. They sat close, his arm around her shoulders, reassuring, but scant protection against a gun.

I crossed to my armchair, leaving Leslie standing in the doorway.

"It might save us all some time and the rest of you some anxiety if we get things straight. Mrs. Bradford will be coming with us. She will be treated with the utmost courtesy. She will

not be harmed. I know everyone in the room is far more concerned about her safety than seeing the three of us caught.
Therefore you will let us drive to Toronto without alerting the
police. It's that simple. We will leave Mrs. Bradford in a safe
place along with Mr. Townsend's car, which will also remain
unharmed." He nodded his head in my direction. "Mr. Chadwick has already suggested an alternate plan whereby we would
take him as our hostage."

"Geoffry," said Catherine, then lapsed into silence, a silence
humming with words. I knew she was too shy to speak. From
across the room I smiled at Catherine as Sir William Fitzralph
gaved impassively onto the scene.

"But we do not want a male hostage," continue Leslie,
patiently, as though he were explaining fire-drill procedures to
a group of slow learners. "A man could give us trouble. A woman
won't risk taking on three armed men."

"That's the most chauvinistic remark I've ever heard!" Madge
banged her fist on the arm of her chair. "When I was younger,
I could have taken on any three men, better armed than you, I
might add, and I would have left them all exhausted."

"Atta boy, girl!" exclaimed Larry.

Leslie ignored the interruption. "We don't want anyone old
enough to possibly need medical attention." He aimed his
glasses at Harriet. "And we don't want to play word games all
the way to Toronto."

"Very well," said Madge rising to her feet. "In that case I will
go and make sandwiches for you to take along. Mark, if you
come and sit here; Harriet, over there, then Catherine can put
her feet up for a few minutes. It's going to be a long session for
her. Larry, you come and help me. I know where things are in

the kitchen, but I have trouble cutting stuff. My right wrist is full of arthritis. Mikos, you're on."

Picking up her purse she filed out of the room followed by Larry and Mikos. Larry had obviously replenished his tumbler while I was in the kitchen. I could see it was almost full as he carried it with him down the hall.

Leslie and Jean-Guy sat facing into the room. Through the window overlooking the lake I could see ominous black clouds beginning to marshal themselves on the horizon. I remembered from previous visits to the lake how quickly storms can blow up. A bright and sun-drenched morning is no guarantee of a cinerama sunset. In fact the sun had just about given up trying to penetrate the dense, dark mass. Twilight would descend much earlier, and with it the enforced departure of Catherine. And there seemed at the moment to be little anyone could do.

From where I sat I could see the far side of the lake where white sails headed towards shore. It had been a busy afternoon on the water, the warm weather of the first long holiday weekend had dotted the lake with sailboats, launches, outboard motors, even rowboats and canoes. Most now headed for shelter as gusts of wind churned the surface of the water into waves on which the occasional whitecap exploded into spume.

From my vantage point, stage left of the fireplace, I could see down the hallway to the kitchen. Madge stood at the counter beside the sink, her back to me, apparently buttering slices of bread. Beside her Larry stood cutting what looked like a small tinned ham. From the corner of her mouth, fully visible from where I sat, dangled a lighted cigarette. Quite obviously she had extra packages in her bag.

I was too far away to hear what they were saying, but I did

see Larry turn around and look at Mikos, out of sight around the corner. The look was a real sizzler.

By now I figured Larry to be really drunk; the signs were becoming all too clear.

Catherine moved slowly towards the couch and sat. "Mark, Geoffry, I know you're both worried about me, but I'm going to be all right. They mean no harm. I am simply going to be a passenger in a car heading to Toronto. I'll be bored, but I will be O.K. And as soon as they let me go, I'll call." She smiled wanly at me. "This really wasn't the weekend I had in mind, Geoffry. I hope you'll give me another chance."

She sat back on the couch, swung her feet up, and lay with her right arm across her eyes. In a low voice Harriet asked Catherine if she would like something to cover her. Catherine raised her arm and shook her head.

The rest of us sat slumped in our chairs. Fatigue and boredom and anxiety had moved us way beyond bridge and Bump and charades and In The Manner Of. Random sentences on a piece of paper could in no way raise our collective spirits as we sat, so many deflated inner tubes, waiting for Catherine to be taken away.

I glanced up at Mark, across the room. He now sat in the chair vacated by Madge, facing the fireplace just inside the door leading to the front hall. He caught my gaze and gave a half-smile along with a wave of his hand. To my chagrin I remembered that same gesture from long ago. I made a sign of acknowledgment, and in the heavy silence I found myself invaded by memory . . . .

There are certain experiences in life one believes will never end, when time stands arrested: a live performance of *Parsifal*,

or a long distance telephone call when you are in the middle of
sex. I might also add to this list the aftermath of a love affair,
as one moves through a continuous present, still shackled to the
past, ignorant of the future.

By a curious irony the beginning of a love affair unfolds in
this same continuous present. The past disappears; the future
beckons, but has no shape. The lovers move through an un-
ending here and now, unencumbered by anything but the
moment. After walking away from Mark on the mountain I
found myself once again trapped in the present, an insect in
amber.

It would have been comforting to be able to say, "My heart
is broken." I was younger then, and clichés could still console.
But the heart is a resilient muscle. It can bruise, tear, falter, but
not break. Bones break; the heart does not.

Furthermore, love had not ended. The presence was gone,
but not the emotion. I had not been exiled from that green and
gold romance landscape of the mind. We had not stagnated in
indifference nor mired ourselves in misunderstanding. But we
stood on opposite sides of a chasm, impossible to bridge, our
voices disintegrating into echo. The love affair had not ended;
it had stopped.

Hope is like a whore, promising everything and delivering
nothing but a cold hole for which you have to pay. I had been
naïve enough to hope that Mark would come to see the error
of his ways and look me up. I had meant what I had said about
leaving him; I did not intend to seek him out. But were he to
have telephoned suggesting dinner, I knew I would have accepted.

But he did not telephone. I had no word from him, nor of
him from such of our mutual friends as I occasionally saw. And

I could not bring myself to ask. I was at sixes and sevens with Geoffry Chadwick far more than with Mark Crosby. I longed to see him but refused to allow the tiniest concession to make a meeting probable, even possible. At the same time I was cutting quite a swath through the bars, tricking up a storm, and using my quote-unquote broken heart as a club to beat off any attempt at intimacy beyond straightforward promiscuity. At the time I thought I was miserable; now I realize I was having a pretty good time.

One Sunday afternoon the following February, I left my apartment in a fit of restlessness, anxious to get out but having no particular destination in mind. It was clear but very cold.

I walked along Sherbrooke Street into a cutting east wind to find myself in front of the museum. I climbed the long flight of steps up to the front door, steps which turn a repository for paintings into a temple of art. Inside the building I checked my overshoes and coat, then headed up yet another majestic staircase to where the objects of art were housed. Visiting a museum is similar to revisiting one's childhood. Look but don't touch!

Sometimes, on a Sunday afternoon, the museum is a pretty good place to cruise. It was in the middle forefront of my mind that I might pick up a graduate student in art history for a quickie. Then I saw Mark. For a fragment of a second I hesitated, the urge to flee paralyzed by the physical jolt of seeing him. He turned, looked across the large hall, and hooked me with a glance. Quickly he crossed over to me.

"Geoffry!" he proferred his hand to shake.

My reflexes had gone into reverse. It took me a second to absorb the idea that I was to grasp his right hand and pump it up and down, not go at him like a Sumo wrestler.

"Hi, Mark, read any good books lately?"

He half-smiled, and reached up to rub his left ear lobe, a gesture I remembered he used to make when uncomfortable. A gold band circled the fourth finger of his left hand.

"Is that a wedding ring? Or has your signet ring turned itself around?"

"It's a wedding ring. I called several times to tell you, but there was no answer."

"I've been out a lot."

"It all happened rather suddenly, actually."

"So it would seem. Where is the new Mrs. Crosby?"

"She's – powdering her nose."

"Is she going to powder the seat too?"

Mark laughed out loud. "Holy Christ, Geoffry, you haven't changed, have you!"

"There's no butterfly lurking inside this caterpillar, Mark. I suppose congratulations are in order. It is just that I have never considered marriage a real achievement, outside of nineteenth-century fiction. And now, as they say, I really must dash."

"Won't you wait and meet Mona?"

"Mona! As in Mauna Loa?"

"No, as in Mona McCutcheon."

"Some other time, Mark. One body blow at a time. And I'm really not up to Mark and Mona right now; I've just eaten. See you later."

I should have turned right then and walked away, but I stupidly hesitated. Mark gave another of his half-smiles and a small wave, with the hand wearing the ring, naturally, and I realized my feelings for him had not changed.

From the corner of my eye I saw a female form crossing the

large room with immense purpose and heading in our direction.

"I must say, Mark, you make a beautiful bridegroom. And now, *au revoir, mon ami.*"

"So long, Geoffry. See you around."

"That's where I'll be: around."

I ducked out of the gallery and fled down the stairs, two at a time. The woman in the checkroom gave me a quizzical look; I had only just arrived.

The cold February air struck me with impact as I began to walk away. Mark was now a married man, and that was the end of that. I used to do one of two things when I was in this kind of funk: go to the movies or go to the baths. On this cold Sunday afternoon I chose the baths, where I spent several hours frolicking in the steam room until my pores were so wide open they yawned.

Afterwards, I dragged myself home, fell exhausted into bed, and slept right through the Monday-morning alarm. Life went on; it always does. One learns to live with a closed door; one has to.

A couple of months later I went to a dreadful party where I met Peter Piper and his record collection. By fall I had left Peter and, to my surprise, made the discovery that I had left Mark as well.

XII

The sight of Madge coming down the hall followed by Larry and Mikos pulled me back into the present. Madge walked as if down a ramp. Still the showgirl, she carried herself as though her pant-suit were a body-stocking sprinkled with bugle beads and three ostrich plumes towered above her head. Although conservative myself about clothes, I deeply admire women who refuse to succumb to the grandmother image. I believe all hair nets, pin-on lace collars, and medium-heeled black oxfords which tie over the instep, should be burned in the public square by the hangman, along with knitting bags and cardigans held in place with alligator clamps joined by a string of fake pearls.

Madge came into the living room and stood looking around hesitantly, as all the comfortable chairs were occupied.

"Please sit down, ma'am," said Leslie.

" ' "Shoot if you must this old grey head. But spare your country's flag," she said,' " Madge declaimed.

At that moment Catherine swung her feet onto the floor and indicated with a gesture that Madge was to sit beside her.

"I'd put my feet back up, if I were you, hon," said Madge as she headed towards one of the straight-backed chairs in front of the fireplace.

"No, no. Come and sit here. I'm way too tense to relax."

"Would you like a Valium? I'm sure I have one in here

somewhere." Madge peered into the recesses of her straw bag.

"No, thanks," said Catherine. "Just the motion of the car will make me dopey enough without extra help."

"What you need is a good strong cup of tea!" announced Harriet. I could tell she was the kind of woman who would have prescribed a cup of tea or good fresh air for any ailment from pre-menstrual tension to leprosy.

"No, thanks, I couldn't drink any more tea at the moment."

While this exchange was going on I could see Larry had paused in front of the bathroom, not surprisingly as gin is the most powerful diuretic in the world next to stage-fright. Larry whispered to Mikos, then stepped into the bathroom and out of my line of vision. Mikos glanced around, hesitated for just a second, then followed Larry into the bathroom. The door shut soundlessly.

I sat staring stupidly down the hallway, my brain stubbornly refusing to accept the evidence offered by my eyes. Larry and Mikos were shut in the bathroom obviously getting it on. I knew Larry had pulled some bizarre stunts in the past, but this was a new high, or low. At least when he used to work the confessionals the priests were not holding him hostage. But right under everybody's nose he was about to give one of our captors a blowjob. I have heard that over a period of time hostages come to identify strongly with their captors, but to fellate a felon vastly exceeds the bounds of taste. I made a solemn private vow that if we got out of this one alive I was going to take Lawrence Townsend II outside and kick his ass until his ears rang.

As if reading my stupefied stare, and realizing that Larry and Mikos had not reentered the room, Leslie turned to look down the hall. "Where are they?" he said, to no one in particular.

Seated beside him, Jean-Guy turned to look.

"They are in the john," I replied, my voice just barely audible, although why I was being so tactful I don't really know. "I don't think they want to be disturbed."

Even Leslie, sharp as he was, did not catch on at once. Madge did, and almost but not quite managed to stifle a snort of laughter.

"What is going on?" demanded Nigel, his question rising not from curiosity but from a wish to deny his impotence in the present situation.

"I don't think you really want to know."

"Of course I want to know!"

"Larry and Mikos are locked in the bathroom having oral sex. It's dark and lonely work, but I suppose somebody has to do it."

"I don't believe it!"

"Somehow I suspected you'd say that."

"Jesus Christ!" muttered Leslie as he sprang from his chair and raced down the hall.

It occurred to me that was the first time I had heard him swear.

With the bottom of his fist he pounded on the bathroom door. "What the hell is going on in there?"

A ripple of reaction spread around the room, but I was far too preoccupied with the bathroom door to pay attention. Leslie thumped the door a second time. In the almost tactile silence that had fallen over the room I heard sounds from inside the bathroom: a thud, a loud cry, whether of pain or sexual pleasure I could not tell, followed by a clatter, as if a hard object had fallen into the bathtub. Then a pause, of absolute, dead silence.

The bathroom door opened slowly, so slowly the friction of the hinges was clearly audible. Astonishment caused Leslie to take two steps backward. Through the door, his two hands resting on top of his head, stepped Mikos. He turned, bringing him into eye contact with Leslie. Holding Mikos' pistol, Larry stepped through the bathroom door to stand behind Mikos.

Shielded by his prisoner's body from the other two armed men, Larry spoke. "You had better do exactly what I say or I will shoot your friend. Nothing personal I assure you. Finest piece of equipment I ever saw. But I am a very nervous girl. Leslie, you and Jean-Guy will hand your guns to Mr. Chadwick. You will move very slowly. I repeat: I'm a very nervous girl."

Nobody moved. We could all have been figures in a wax museum.

"Mr. Townsend," said Leslie softly, "you are not a killer. You could not shoot a person in cold blood. I could, and will. Now please. Just hand the gun back to Mikos and come and sit down."

At the risk of sounding like a coward, I had an overpowering urge to duck behind my armchair. If bullets started to fly I was right in the line of fire. But any kind of abrupt movement could easily prove fatal.

"Perhaps I'm not a killer in everyday life," replied Larry. "But I'm pissed to the gills and that's the next best thing. And if you take our hostess away, who's going to cook our dinner? Geoffry, Mark, please take the guns."

"Don't anybody move!" hissed Leslie.

I looked at Leslie; I looked at the Magnum; I looked at Jean-Guy who had his pistol trained nervously on the room. I did not move. Nor did anyone else.

"This is becoming very bo-ring," sang Larry. "Tell you what. Leslie place your weapon on the floor. Jean-Guy will do like-wise. Geoffry, you will pick them up."

"You stupid idiot," snarled Leslie. "Risking our entire plan over . . . *Christ!*"

I presumed he was speaking to Mikos.

"Mr. Townsend – " Leslie raised his voice – "if necessary I will shoot Mikos. Then I will shoot you. Now, very slowly, hand your gun to me." Slowly Leslie raised his weapon until it was aimed at Mikos' chest.

"No!" cried Mikos, speaking for the first time.

"Oh, deary me!" exclaimed Larry. "Why is it that no one will ever take an old fairy seriously?"

From behind the shield of Mikos' body I could see Larry take aim at Leslie, and thereby at me. Were he to fire and miss I was there to keep the bullet from damaging the upholstery. I have been happier.

Slowly, Jean-Guy leaned over and placed his pistol on the floor in front of him. I made no move to pick it up.

Why is it that under moments of extreme stress and tension our minds often leap away from the crisis at hand to focus on something seemingly irrelevant. For some odd reason I found myself thinking of *Tosca*. Towards the end of Act II, in order to save her lover's life, Tosca agrees to put out for the wicked chief of police, Scarpia. While he is engaged in writing out a safe conduct, she crosses to the dinner table for a little restorative wine. In doing so she sees a knife on a plate; and, in what is usually a criminally shocking bit of overacting, she conceals the knife behind her back in order to dispatch the villain.

Suddenly the irrelevant turned relevant as, on the edge of my field of vision, the lemon meringue pie came into focus. Surely God had put it there on the coffeetable, within reach, for a purpose. Crazy, dangerous, utterly stupid, I knew, but a sudden rush of adrenalin pulled me taut as a guitar string and knocked out commonsense.

"Mr. Townsend, I will count to three: one . . ."

On the count of two, I moved. With a smooth, easy gesture, reminiscent of the tennis serve I had spent my teens perfecting, I scooped up Harriet's pie and aimed it at Leslie. My movement caught his attention and he turned his head just in time to catch the lemon meringue full face as it sailed through the door. At that precise second, Mikos dropped to his knees, a reflex which probably saved his life, as the impact of the pie caused Leslie to fire.

"My God! My pie!" wailed Harriet.

Larry took the bullet in his right shoulder. "Shit!" he hollered as the pistol flew from his grasp, clattering across the hardwood floor to land at Leslie's feet.

I stepped around the table and kicked the pistol lying at Jean-Guy's feet between the two logs. Mark's reflexes were sharp. In a second he had snatched up the pistol and trained it on Leslie.

But although Leslie had taken the impact of the lemon meringue full face, his eyes had been protected by the mirrored glasses. With his left hand he pulled them off and shoved them into a pocket. Then swiftly, gracefully, without taking his eyes off Mark, he scooped up Mikos' pistol at his feet.

Christ! Had I ever blown it! Even now I cannot be entirely sure of why I thought a face full of lemon curd would render Leslie powerless, like a vampire confronted by garlic; but it seemed like a good idea at the time. Most mistakes do.

As it now stood, Leslie had two guns trained on Mark. Larry had been shot. Mark stood in grave danger; a civilized man holding a pistol faced a coolly calculating man holding both a pistol and a Magnum.

"Leslie, a word." As I spoke I moved to stand in front of Mark. I am no hero, but I am prepared to face the consequences of my actions. "Mark, please put down the gun." I faced Leslie as I spoke. "Leslie, you must believe me. I'm sorry for messing up your clothes."

"No problem, Mr. Chadwick, no problem at all. Now, Mr. Crosby, please place your gun on the floor."

"Mark, do as he says. I would prefer not to get shot. Mark – Goddammit!"

"Mark – please!" entreated Catherine.

From the corner of my eye I could see Mark crouch to place the pistol at arm's length on the carpet.

Still on the floor beside Larry, who was slumped against the wall with a hand over his bleeding shoulder, Mikos began to get to his feet.

"Stay where you are," spat Leslie. The Magnum jumped in his hand. Then he turned back to me. "Mr. Chadwick, in spite of yourself you have just done me a considerable favour. I can now unload these two idiots who nearly screwed up my plan. Jean-Guy staked out the wrong house for us to hide out in. Mikos couldn't keep his zipper done up. And thanks to you, I am rid of them both."

With his left hand he slid the pistol into his trouser pocket, still holding the Magnum in his right. From a rear pocket he pulled a handkerchief which he used to wipe his face clean of Harriet's viscous lemon pie.

"And now, Mr. Chadwick, listen carefully. Slowly, very slowly, you will pick up the pistol near Mr. Crosby by the barrel and hand it to me. One trick and I'll blow you away."

I had every confidence he meant what he said. Carefully I

kneeled and reached gingerly for the weapon, turning it with my forefinger until the barrel pointed at my feet. Closing my fingers around the cold metal cylinder I stood and moved toward Leslie, my arm outstretched. With his left hand he took the gun from me.

"Good. Now go and stand beside Mr. Crosby."

I did as I was told. Leslie slid the second pistol into the pocket of his windbreaker.

"Guy, the keys to the Mercedes." He held out his hand. "Come on. Fast. Or I'll shoot you and take them."

Reluctantly, Jean-Guy reached into his pocket. "You're not leaving us behind?" he asked incredulously as he placed a handful of car keys on the table.

"You've got it." Still keeping him covered, Leslie reached for the keys to the Mercedes-Benz, attached to a ring with a Mercedes logo. "And now, *au revoir*, Mrs. Bradford, you will remain here. I can move faster alone. I apologize for the inconvenience, and most especially for the dogs. Mr. Chadwick, perhaps we may meet again one day, under different circumstances. Please don't anyone follow me or I will shoot to kill!"

With that he reached around the doorway, still keeping us all covered, scooped up the packsack containing the money, and dashed through the front door. Seconds later, the rasp of tires on gravel announced his departure at a fast clip up the driveway in Madge's orange Datsun.

"Damn!" exclaimed Madge as through the window she watched her car disappear from sight. "I always leave the keys in the ignition, in case someone wants to get in or out. And that sidewinder has stolen my car. Oh, well, at least I can smoke." She fished around in her bag for cigarettes.

Leslie may have taken off with traces of lemon pie on his face, but Jean-Guy and Mikos both had egg on theirs. Stranded, unarmed, outnumbered, the captors were well on their way to becoming captive.

"*Hostie!*" muttered Jean-Guy under his breath as he stood irresolute behind the coffeetable.

By now Mikos had scrambled to his feet. He looked just as unfocussed as did his elongated colleague. Suddenly he moved to stand beside Jean-Guy. From one of the zippered pockets in his jacket he took out a switchblade and pressed the catch. The knife opened with a click. I took a couple of steps backwards just as Mark crossed to the fireplace and grabbed the poker from its stand. Holding it in two hands like a baseball bat he stepped in front of me, followed by Nigel, who grabbed the matching shovel and held it like a cricket bat.

In spite of the reality of this confrontation I could not help thinking there was something almost slapstick about the scene, with Mutt and Jeff faced off against the Rover Boys. The rest of the ex-hostages had moved to the other side of the room. For a few moments we stood in freeze-frame. I knew we had to diffuse the situation, to get Jean-Guy and Mikos out of the way so we could get Larry to the hospital.

"Hold it everybody!" I took two steps forward and raised my arms in front of Mark and Nigel in a gesture of restraint. "Mikos, Jean-Guy, why don't you just clear out? Your quarrel is not with us but with Leslie, who has just shafted you both. You are outnumbered. Now, before anyone else gets hurt just go."

They stood still, trapped by indecision.

"Look, you have two choices. Either you can make a run for it and try to drop out of sight, or you can give yourselves up to the police and hope they'll take that into consideration."

I have been told I have natural authority. As I looked at the knife Mikos held I hoped it was true. Mikos looked at Jean-Guy, who nodded his head sideways towards the door. Carefully they edged out from behind the table. Jean-Guy scooped up all the car keys and headed for the front door as Mikos, still holding the knife defensively in front of him, backed out of the living room. After making one last threatening gesture with his switchblade he turned to follow Jean-Guy through the door.

In a second I had locked the front door from the inside. "Mark, get the porch door," I ordered.

Halfway up the stairs to the landing, directly above the front door, was a large, fan-shaped window. Taking the stairs two at a time, I looked out to see what the two baffled hoods would do. It was then I realized why Leslie had demanded the keys to the Mercedes. Parked where it was, just outside the front door, it effectively blocked all the other cars. The driveway lay only a few feet from the house, making it impossible to manoeuvre a car between the house and the Mercedes; while the far side of the driveway was defined by a dry-stone wall about two feet high. There was no possible way to get any of the cars out of the driveway without first moving the Mercedes.

I suppose a truly resourceful criminal would know how to start a car by jumping the wires, but this solution did not present itself to these two amateurs. From my vantage point above the front door I could see a hurried consultation, the outcome of which seemed to be that to separate would offer them a better chance of getting away than hanging together. Jean-Guy took off up the driveway with the fast lope of an ostrich, while Mikos appeared to cut down towards the shoreline around the side of the house and out of my line of vision.

With the abrupt departure of our univited guests the house began to hum with activity. Catherine kneeled beside Larry to slide a cushion under his head and staunch his wound with a towel. He lay on the floor unconscious, whether from shock or liquor I could not tell.

"Better call the police at once," I said.

"And an ambulance," added Catherine. "I could drive him to the hospital, but I don't know how badly he's hurt. He'd better go on a stretcher."

Mark dialled the provincial police, tersely ordering them to send a patrol car and an ambulance, and to look out for an orange Datsun. Here Madge handed him a slip of paper on which she had jotted down the license number of her car.

There seemed nothing further to do but wait.

"How far do you suppose they'll get?" I asked Madge.

"It's hard to say. They're not exactly the most heads-up act I've ever seen. I guess they didn't stop and give a coin to a blind beggar after the heist."

"I say," honked Nigel from his vantage point in front of the window overlooking the lake. That Mikos blighter has taken our skiff."

Madge and I hurried to the window in time to see Mikos grappling with oars as the skiff in question made its erratic way from the beach towards a small point of land jutting out from the shoreline. Rowing is not nearly as easy as it looks, and Mikos could not get the knack of pulling evenly on the oars. The black clouds were beginning to dissipate as quickly as they had blown up, but the wind held steady and kept blowing him off course. Gradually the small boat bobbed its way out of sight around the point.

"This really is too much!" Harriet's voice took on a new note of shrill exasperation. "First you ruin my pie, and then your beastly bank robbers steal our skiff. How are we supposed to get home?"

I should have kept my mouth shut; I am old enough to know better. But a sudden wave of such intense irritation flooded through me that had the pie still been on the table I probably would have thrown it at Harriet.

"They are not 'our' bank robbers, as you so charmingly put it. And the next time you bring a pie to a hostage-taking make sure it's coconut cream. As for getting home, I am sure Catherine and Mark could lend you each a bathingsuit."

High outrage rendered Harriet Walford temporarily speechless. It was probably just as well. Through the pin-drop silence we all grew aware of an unhealthy wheezing sound and turned our collective heads to see Mr. Bradford having a seizure of some sort on the seat in front of the bow window.

"Ohmygod!" whispered Catherine. "He's having a heart attack."

"Loosen his ascot and cover him," ordered Harriet. For once she did not prescribe tea.

"Mark, Nigel," I said, "come and help me push the Mercedes out of the way. Then we can move the other cars so as not to block the ambulance when it comes.

"Jolly good idea!" replied Nigel.

The three of us managed to push the Mercedes back past the front door and onto the lawn out of the way. Catherine and Mark had spare keys for their cars, and I always carry an extra set of apartment and car keys in my shaving kit. I once suggested to Larry that having extra keys was a good idea, and to my astonishment he agreed. I'd even told him where I kept mine. As luck would have it I managed to dig spare keys for his Olds from a shaving kit which looked more like a cosmetic case. In short order we had moved Catherine's station-wagon and Larry's Olds onto the grassy centre of the loop formed by the driveway, and backed my Cadillac and Mark's Volvo onto the lawn beside the Mercedes-Benz.

"Looks like we're going to have a fine sunset," observed Nigel as we headed back towards the house. "Can't beat a sunset in the country."

"Try neon lights in the city," I replied as I reached for the doorknob.

We went inside.

XIII

The house really looked lived in. Larry lay in the hall leading to the kitchen, a pillow under his head, a blanket covering him. Bits of meringue and lemon filling dotted the small Indian rug and surrounding hardwood floor. On the window-seat a slate-grey Mr. Bradford moaned softly, obviously in great pain. He belonged to that generation of stiff-upper-lippers who looked on illness as shameful. To reveal symptoms of any sort in public was downright rude. They suppressed sneezes, swallowed burps, and treated heart attacks as if they were mild bouts of indigestion. And when confronted by the inescapable fact of another person in physical distress they discreetly looked the other way.

Catherine cradled her father's head, promising that any minute the ambulance would arrive, bringing ease. Mark stood next to her. I don't think I have ever felt more genuine admiration for another human being than I felt for Catherine at that moment. Having just been subjected to an afternoon that would take the curl out of anybody's hair, she remained the strong and nurturing figure. And were I given to the self-indulgence of envy, I could have envied Mark for being married to this remarkable woman.

Madge sat quietly beside Catherine and Mark. The Walfords stood about, taking up space, blocking out the light, breathing up the air, useless but bursting to be of use.

Ten minutes passed. Nigel had moved to take up a position
"at ease" by the front door. "I believe they are here," he announced. By now Harriet had retreated to the kitchen to make
tea. Sure enough, a police car followed by an ambulance was
coming down the driveway. I don't think that in my entire life
I have seen a more welcome sight.

There followed a general exodus. In short order, Mr.
Bradford and Larry were lifted into the ambulance which took
off without delay. Fortunately the nearby town was large enough
to rate a hospital. Catherine rode along with her father.

After piecing together a statement from Mark and me, the
officer in charge managed to get a description of the three men
in spite of interference by Nigel, who kept insisting that the
windbreaker was grey, not green. "I'm certain it was grey.
Wouldn't you have called it grey, Harriet?"

I motioned the officer outside and gave him a final and
accurate description of the three fugitives. From his car the
officer radioed for a helicopter to search for a skiff whose sole
occupant was dressed in black leather. He also put out an alert
for an unusually tall man on foot in a sage-green windbreaker.
I gave the officer my business card and promised to make myself
available. That seemed to wrap it up for the time being. He got
into his car and drove off after arranging with Mark to have the
Mercedes towed away.

The weather remained unsettled and the wind high. By now
the water had become really rough; foot-high waves frothed
with whitecaps. Even if the skiff had not been stolen, for the
Walfords to attempt to row home would have been heroic, not

to say foolhardy. I wondered what sort of progress Mikos was making, an inexperienced oarsman trying to control a lightweight boat in a high wind.

Harriet Walford, now playing the impatient wife, demanded to be taken home. It was decided the Walfords would borrow the station-wagon to return home for the night. They left in a volley of commonplaces. Wasn't it dreadful! You will let us know the very second. The poor dear. I really can't get over it. Who would have thought? Whatever is the world coming to. And so forth. Jesus! Was I glad to see them go.

I could tell Madge was the kind of woman for whom an automobile was as necessary to survival as eyeglasses or cigarettes. For any trip over one hundred yards I would be willing to bet she slid behind the wheel. I suggested she borrow Larry's car. He certainly would not be driving for a while.

"Are you going to be all right?" asked Mark. "If you're apprehensive about going home you could stay here."

"Thanks, sweetie, but I'll be O.K. Nobody wants anything from an old broad, more's the pity. I'll pop a couple of downers and hit the hay. Let me know the minute you hear about Roger. Wake me, if necessary. The phone is right beside my bed. Are the keys in the ignition?"

"Yes, we left them there," I replied. "And, Madge, this time don't leave anything behind."

"Right on." She gave a small chuckle. "Well, as they say: it's been surreal."

Mark and I stood in the doorway watching her walk to Larry's car.

"She's far too peppy for your father-in-law," I observed. "Even before the heart attack."

"Isn't she just. But speaking of my father-in-law, I had better get into town. Want to come along?"

"No, thanks. I hate hospitals. I'm not a hand wringer. I suppose I should keep a midnight vigil at the bedside of Larry, my oldest and dearest friend. But he won't die. He's far too selfish. I'll just stay here and wait for Elizabeth and Robert so I can fill them in on what's happened."

"Probably a good idea. I'll let you know as soon as anything breaks." He climbed into his car and drove off.

I was wonderfully, blessedly alone. Twilight was beginning to fall, and the grey sky glowed with a soft luminosity.

In the lingering light I buried the dogs.

By the time I had finished filling in the trench, I was sweating profusely. In my room I stripped and went into the bathroom to shower. On the floor under the handbasin lay the crypto chopping board with that abominable poem telling city folks not to throw tampons into the toilet. Putting one and two together I figured Larry must have enticed Mikos into taking his pants down. In order to peel down those skin-tight leather trousers he would have had to put down his gun. While he was thus occupied, Larry must have clobbered him with the chopping board before grabbing the weapon. That he might have been shot dead for his temerity probably didn't occur to Larry. His limited sense of discretion is always knocked out by liquor.

Towelling myself dry, I put on fresh clothes, meaning my other non-formal clean shirt, an unbleached cotton job, almost but not quite white, with a button-down collar. Then I poured myself a generous shot of Black Label to which I added just enough water to ease my conscience. I turned on lights and straightened up the living room, putting the straight-backed chairs around the dining room table and carrying used teacups and glasses out to the kitchen. I folded up the card table and emptied Madge's ashtray.

After doing my best to pick up crumbled meringue from the hall floor and to sponge away traces of the lemon filling from the rug, I noticed a couple of dark smudges which served as a grim reminder of the dead dogs who had lain there. Even though the floor is getting farther and farther away with each passing year, I kneeled down, rolled the rug into a neat cylinder, and carried it out to the sunporch to be dispatched to the cleaners. Short of tackling the windows or washing walls I had run out of chores.

I carried my drink out to the porch where, screened from the wind, I could hear the waves as they spilled over the pebbled beach. It had been, to say the very least, a curious afternoon. I wondered how long it would be before Mikos and Jean-Guy were picked up. It is not hard to spot the Eiffel Tower, even wearing a windbreaker. And Mikos was dressed with such urban anti-chic that in a rural area he would be doubly conspicuous. That is, unless he had been tipped out of the boat by waves, possibly drowned. But he appeared to have been following the shoreline, and the prevailing wind was still strong enough to keep him from crossing the lake.

Leslie was the one who caused me some thought. I stood, sipping my highball and trying to decide whether or not I really wanted him to be caught. Not surprisingly the socially conscious lawyer, Geoffry Chadwick, wanted the armed robber, hostage-taker, and potential kidnapper apprehended and brought to justice. Without legal restraints our society as we know it would soon disintegrate into chaos. However, there was a part of me wishing wholeheartedly that Leslie would get away, and with the loot. This same voice told me to applaud the audacity and initiative, the sheer moxie of organizing a bank robbery, pulling it off, and then holding a middle-class microcosm at gunpoint for an entire afternoon.

Furthermore, who am I to pass judgement? Like most people I have shadowy pockets in my past, things done I dearly hope will never see the light of day. "When that One Great Scorer comes to write against our names" he is going to discover that most of us, at one time or another, have run afoul of the Criminal Code. Only many of us are lucky and don't get caught.

I was also flooded with relief that the robbers had left before Elizabeth and Robert returned from their outing. Had they been absorbed into the group of hostages, the balance might have shifted, the outcome have been different. They might even have decided to take Elizabeth along with them. She is younger and less self-possessed than Catherine, more easily intimidated and controlled.

The idea of telephoning my sister Mildred to tell her that Elizabeth was on her way back to Toronto in a car with three armed robbers was not one I even wanted to contemplate. To be fair to Mildred, she would have been genuinely concerned about her daughter's safety. She would also have fretted about Elizabeth's underwear. Just supposing Elizabeth had been shot dead and the coroner had to perform an autopsy and discovered that Elizabeth's underwear was full of holes. Mildred could never have lived with the shame.

By now I had finished my drink. I went back inside the house and poured myself another. I was just on my way to the kitchen for a splash of water when I hear wheels crunch on the driveway. I walked to the front door, bracing myself to tell Robert and Elizabeth what had happened during their absence. But it was Mark who stepped out of the car.

"Is there a drop left in the bottle for me?" he asked.

"A small one," I replied, standing aside to let him into the house.

He passed me and went directly to the bar, then returned to the living room with his drink. "They put Mr. Bradford into intensive care; we don't know yet for how long. He is conscious, but he's in a great deal of pain. I'd like to get him to Montreal, but I don't know whether he's well enough to make the trip. We just have to sit tight for the moment."

"And Larry?"

"Sedated, but all right. The bullet only grazed the bone. He lost blood, and for some time he's going to have a very sore arm. Otherwise he'll be fine."

"Where's Catherine?"

"She's spending the night with friends who live not far from the hospital. She wants to be on hand in case there is any real change in her father's condition. She told me to come back and look after you."

"That's good of her, but I really don't need looking after. You may prefer to go back to town."

"No point really. I'd only be underfoot. And just between us I find the people Catherine is staying with make pretty heavy weather."

"Do you know anybody in the country, outside of Madge, who doesn't?"

Mark gave a small laugh. "You mean Nigel and Harriet? Fortunately they don't come over to our side of the lake very often." He had finished his drink in about four swallows and stood uncertainly rubbing the back of his neck. "I suppose I should go and finish burying the dogs before Catherine gets back tomorrow. I'll do the digging if you hold the flashlight."

"It's all done. I buried them while you were gone."

"Geoffry, you didn't have to do that."

"I know I didn't have to, but I did. And I have the blisters to prove it. The spot will need rolling, possibly more fill, and new sod. But they are out of sight, if not out of mind."

He shook his head. "You really are something else. I'll go and take a shower. Then I'll rustle us up something to eat."

"I'm not really hungry. I'd far sooner drink."

"Any word from Robert and Elizabeth?"

"Nope. Maybe we should call them. Do you have the number?"

"Yes."

"Why don't I call while you take your shower."

Mark went upstairs, and I dialled the number he had given me. A breathy voice came onto the line to tell me that the younger members of the party, including Robert and Elizabeth, had piled into a car and driven off to the far end of the lake, which happened to be in the United States. I thanked the voice on the telephone and rang off, unwilling to get into explanations. Sooner or later the two of them would show up and find out about all the fun they had missed.

As I poured myself another drink I could hear the water running upstairs. With just the faintest twinge of apprehension I realized that I was alone in the house with Mark.

XIV

Mark had never been one to spend much time "making his toilet," as the French would say. So fearful was he to be thought vain about his appearance that I could have measured the time he spent in the bathroom with an egg timer. When I first knew him he was addicted to Lifebuoy soap, which in those days reeked of carbolic acid. No bar of Cashmere Bouquet ever touched his body, and he even mistrusted Lux as it was supposedly favoured by most of the female Hollywood stars. After a while, I stopped giving him aftershave lotion. The unopened bottles sat in a row in the medicine cabinet like whiskey bottles in a temperance household.

In short order Mark bounded down the stairs and into the living room. In the dim light he looked about thirty-five, the bastard. Aside from his supple step and lean figure, he was dressed in that town and country fashion which has been adopted by men from eighteen to eighty. Over a green open-necked shirt he had pulled on a gold sweater with a tiny amphibious creature stitched to the front. Chinos and sandals completed the outfit. And then I caught a whiff, an aroma. Mark was wearing cologne; moreover it was Aramis. On my skin it smells like turpentine. But on someone else? *Caveat emptor.*

I sat in the chair beside the fireplace. Like the bull in the bull ring, secure in his *querencia*, I had staked out this chair as my own.

"You're sure you're not hungry?" asked Mark.

"Not really. When I am I'll get a piece of cheese from the fridge." I was really beginning to feel the effects of my drinks, and I did not want anything as matter-of-fact as food to dull the edge. I waited until he poured himself a fresh drink and sat down across from me.

"How are you? It's been quite an afternoon."

"A bit strung out. Better for a shower and a drink. And you?"

"I'm O.K., I guess. I'm going to be stiff tomorrow from the shovelling, but it will pass. I shall probably have recurring nightmares as a result of that final scene in the hallway. I thought Larry was more likely to shoot me than Leslie, and then my fool-hardy idea of kicking you the other pistol. We're both lucky we didn't get plugged."

"Especially you, stepping in front of me the way you did. I was really impressed."

I shrugged noncommitally. "In a bizarre way, the real hero of the piece is Larry."

Mark smiled. "I guess he is. He certainly faced down the villain and rescued the damsel in distress. By the way, Geoffry, were you on the level when you suggested to Leslie in the kitchen that they take you along as hostage?"

"I thought it a pretty good idea, for them anyway. No one would have thought of looking for them in Westmount, especially when the announced destination was Toronto."

"You were prepared to do that for Catherine?"

"For Catherine and you. Face it, if I have to be held hostage, I would sooner be in my own house, with my own books and chair. And at my age there are worse fates than being cooped up with three very nervous young men. Who knows? We might really have got something going."

Mark leaned forward in his chair. "Why is it that you always laugh off anything serious?"

"Survival, pure and simple."

"But if you and Larry hadn't intervened, Catherine would be en route to Toronto. Her safety, even her life, would be in their hands."

"True enough."

"And I would have done anything to prevent her going. So would you, it would seem. I would have shot those bastards, to keep her here."

"The voice of the territorial male."

We fell into an uncomfortable silence. Mark leaned back in his chair, crossed both hands over his abdomen, and stretched out his legs. Almost at once he shifted position, sitting up straight and running his right had through his hair.

"Geoffry, let's go to bed," he blurted out without preamble.

"Let's not," I replied, crossing my legs. "Let's just sit here quietly and get drunk."

"And then go to bed?"

"As they say in Vladivostok: *nyet*, thanks."

"Come on, Geoffry. After all these years? One more time isn't going to kill us."

"I am not feeling sentimental. I said it once and I'll say it again. While I am in Catherine's house as her guest I will not play roll-around with her husband. Nor anywhere else, for that matter."

He stood and crossed to lean one elbow on the mantelpiece, looking down and putting me at a distinct disadvantage. "Why don't we toss a coin? Heads, I win. Tails, you lose."

"Swell, just swell." In order to avoid his magnetic field I stood and moved around the table, in the process giving my shin a sharp and painful bang on the heavy maple slab. "Dammit! Now go and sit down and behave yourself. I do not wish to spend the rest of the evening playing *Private Lives*."

I crossed the room, giving Mark a wide berth, and pushed my way through the door onto the wide porch where I stood looking into darkness, the lake audible but not visible.

Mark followed to stand beside me. Only a four-by-four beam supporting the roof separated us. In a light pleasant baritone he began to sing a Noel Coward waltz. "'I'll see you again, whenever spring breaks through again.'"

"That's *Bitter Sweet*," I observed. "You should be singing, 'Someday I'll find you, moonlight behind you.' However at the moment there isn't any moon, front or back."

Mark struck an attitude, one hand on the pillar, the other on his cheek. " 'Extraordinary how potent cheap music is.' "

"So is expensive whiskey."

" 'What fools we were to ruin it all. What utter, utter fools!' "
We fell into silence.

"Do you remember?" asked Mark. "That was the very first play we saw together."

"Yes, I remember. I remember it well. We went out for dinner afterwards and you sent back your *table d'hôte* and we had a row."

"But we made it up. Did we ever make it up."

"Mark, you're not being very helpful."

"I don't intend to be. I can't understand why you are being so stuffy. Do you think that I love Catherine any less?"

"Mark, spare me that motheaten old argument about constancy being more important than fidelity."

"What I find odd is how we both seem to have done an about face. I was so stiff and conservative when I first knew you, uptight. And you were always trying to loosen me up. Now it's the other way around."

"Has it ever occurred to you that honesty or decency or integrity, or whatever you wish to call it, is efficient? Dishonesty and its subsequent concealment waste a good deal of time. It takes a lot less energy to be straight, no sexual meaning intended. So just in case you think I'm wearing a halo, baby, I can assure you it's only gold-plated."

Even in the dim light I could see him smile. "Do you know what I've noticed about aging homosexuals? They tend to become intensely authoritarian and conservative. They become social Edwardians and political Tories. As for religion they turn into the highest of Anglicans or the most Roman of Catholics. They begin wearing vests, and carrying loose change in a pocket purse, and driving cars with low licence plates. And they adore Lent."

"You have just made a *perçu*. Shall I locate a clay tablet and be your amanuensis. For you information I am still a small 'l' liberal. I eat without using a placemat, I am not constipated, and I know my zip code. And furthermore . . . Christ! We have reached the 'and furthermore' stage, aging homosexuals do not, like aging heteros, have big, messy, mid-life, menopausal love affairs that screw up their marriage of twenty-five years. We have enough of that uncommon commodity known as commonsense to know when and with whom to keep our fly zipped up. And I am growing very tired of this conversation."

"Wait, Geoffry," Mark reached out and put a restraining hand on my arm. His touch disturbed me. "I have another *perçu*.

As you know I had quite a lot of free time on my hands this afternoon. For some reason, I really can't explain, I was looking at the rubbing of Sir William Fitzralph, then at you, then back at the rubbing. And I suddenly realized that under that curmudgeonly exterior beats the heart of a true romantic."

"Bullshit!"

"I'm right, you know. You are a romantic. I don't mean in the sense of fluttering hearts and happy endings. But you believe in rules and codes and the perfectability of man. You're far too intelligent to believe in the Grail, and still there is something in you that hopes to find it. You believe in preserving the past and safeguarding the future. You are an antique, but a wonderful antique. And good antiques must be cherished, and loved. And I am going to get you, Geoffry, because my will to go to bed with you is stronger than yours to refuse. It's that simple."

"If you have finished quoting from your *Reader's Digest Guide to Home Analysis*, Mark, I will replenish my drink. I need the will-power."

Mark made a grab for me as I ducked past him and back into the living room. He followed me through the door. "Here, at least let me be a host and fix you a drink."

Automatically I put my tumbler into his outstretched hand. Instead of going to the bar he put the empty glass onto the mantelpiece.

The next thing, the two of us were on the floor wrestling like a pair of adolescent boys. Not only was I taken totally by surprise, but Mark was the aggressor, giving him a double advantage. As he flipped me onto my back, his face only inches from mine, I was acutely aware of his body beneath the light summer clothing, almost more aware than if he had been naked.

"Mark, let me up. I am a virgin!"

"The hell you are."

"With every full moon I am renewed."

"Cut the poetry, and give up."

"A little yearning is a dangerous thing. And you'll have to kill me first."

We continued to struggle. We are both pretty strong, with the tensile strength of long, not heavy, muscle. But I was nearly five years older and by now a bit drunk. Mark had been right again. His will was stronger. With each passing second it grew harder to fend off his forceful, fragrant presence. I was melting visibly.

With a grunt I pushed him away. I had gotten as far as my knees when he tackled me again. Fortunately the pile of the living room carpet was thick. Again he managed to flip me onto my back, but this time I was lying on my right arm on which he had a firm grip with his left hand.

What the hell, I thought to myself. Why fight city hall?

When he kissed me, I was ready for him. Which is to say I returned his kiss with the same ardour as it was given. It was one of the three or four kisses I will remember when old rocking chair finally gets me.

After a while we came up for air.

"You always did kiss like a vacuum cleaner," murmured Mark.

"These days it's called eating face. I'm not as antique as you think."

The sound of wheels crunching on the driveway brought us scrambling to our feet. We adjusted our clothing, doing our best to conceal our mutual and obvious tumescence.

Robert came bounding through the door, followed by my

niece. "Hey, where is everybody?"

"Go and make yourself a drink," I suggested. "This is going to take a while."

As the two of them went off giggling and whispering to the bar, Mark looked at me, shrugged, and grinned. Then, as if feeling obliged to say something, anything, to break the tension, he said, "She certainly is a beautiful girl, your niece."

"Saved by the belle," I replied.

Even though Elizabeth and Robert had been spared the tedious aspects of the afternoon's events, they were both quite evidently disappointed at having missed the excitement. They sat side by side on the couch, quite literally on the edge of their seats, as Mark and I took turns filling them in on what had been going on. They reminded me of kids who had accidentally missed out on a day's trip to Disneyland.

"Did he actually carry a Magnum?" asked Robert eagerly.

"I couldn't be certain. It looked big enough to blow away an automobile. It killed the dogs instantly."

"Yes, the dogs," repeated Robert thoughtfully as he shook his head. "Those bastards ought to be shot themselves!"

My niece was more interested in the actual events of being held hostage than in the denouement. The thought of those last terrifying seconds made me realize how gladly I would have swapped my experience for hers, the beans and bacon in peace; but no matter how earnestly I might have tried to convince her I knew she would never have believed me.

Still flushed and starry-eyed over their vicarious brush with such raw experience, Elizabeth and Robert went into the kitchen to make themselves a sandwich. I had just poured another drink, Mark having gone upstairs to his bathroom, when Elizabeth came back into the living room to ask if I would like something to eat. My interest in food was still zero.

"Elizabeth," I began without preliminaries, "are you on the Pill?"

The question obviously surprised her. "Yes, why do you ask?"

"Self-preservation. If I deliver you back to my sister the mother and you turn out to be pregnant, I will have to leave not only the country but the North American continent."

"I don't understand." She looked charmingly uncomfortable.

"If you are sleeping with Robert that is your affair. I just want to make sure you can look after yourself."

"What makes you say that?"

"I saw the two of you in bed this morning, over the garage. I was poking about and discovered you quite by accident. I am not passing judgement, Elizabeth; believe me. Your skin is your own business. But your mother telephoned me expressly to ask that I keep an eye on you. So far I have not done a very good job. You were almost taken hostage, and you are sleeping with your host. I won't tell, if you won't. But if you go back to Toronto just a little bit pregnant, then I will be just a little bit dead."

I was under the impression that blushing had gone out of fashion, like cocktail hats or white gloves, but Elizabeth looked hard at the floor while a rush of spanked-baby pink suffused her face and neck.

"Elizabeth, I assure you, I am not saying don't. After seeing my friend wounded and two dogs shot dead I would be a moral moron to oppose something as pro-life as a tumble in the feathers. But you are my niece and, for the nonce, my responsibility.

Robert is a decent young man. Nor, I strongly suspect, does he harbour anything nasty and catching. But he is in 'the prime of his young manhood,' as they say in novels, bad novels; and it takes only one of those teeny-tiny tadpoles to put you on the spot. That's all I have to say. Now go and eat. And nothing for me at the moment, thanks." All pretty confusion, my niece withdrew, to grab a bit to eat followed, no doubt, by a nibble on her host.

Mark was just coming down the stairs when the sound of a car skidding abruptly to a stop drew us both to the front door. Totally unwilling to undergo any more surprises, I was vastly relieved to see the passenger in the taxi was Catherine. But, oddly, she walked right past her husband and threw her arms around my neck. Without a moment's hesitation I wrapped my arms around her body and we stood, for several seconds, rocking one another gently. We did not speak; there was no need.

After a while we separated and she repeated the same wordless routine with Mark. As they drew apart Catherine spoke for the first time. "I don't ordinarily drink this late, but tonight's the night!" With that she marched out to the bar. It occurred to me that her voice was unusually loud. And her colour seemed a bit high.

"How's your father?" I asked after we had regrouped around the fireplace.

"Stable. The doctor assured me there was no need to hang around. And the woman I was to stay with, heart of gold, mouth of brass, wanted to turn the occasion into an all-night, let-it-all-hang-out pyjama party. One of those how-many-times-per-week, is-it-bigger-than-a-breadstick girlie conversations that makes me sick. We had a few drinks, and I decided why waste time talking about it when I had a gorgeous husband waiting at home. I pleaded fatigue and left."

I was beginning to suspect Catherine had popped quite a few drinks before she arrived. My suspicion grew when, without warning, she flung her arms around my neck a second time. "My hero!"

I returned the embrace. More than a little tipsy myself, I was beginning to feel like a sex object and, confidentially, it felt fine.

"You're going to make Goodman Crosby jealous, Goodwife Bradford."

"Don't worry about him. I may be smooching with you, but he's going to reap the benefit. Aren't you, stuff?" She made a lunge for Mark. More than just tight, she was stinko.

"How's Larry?" I asked.

"Out cold. The doctor claims he's sedated, but we all know it's demon rum. The old bugger! He saved me from a fate worse than death, although I guess that's a pretty tacky metaphor under the circs."

"Catherine, dearest," I began. "You look tired." Behind her back I winked broadly at Mark. "You've had a big day. I think it's time for beddy-bye."

"And how!" she replied, grabbing Mark by the wrist. "Come on, hunk. Time to bring a little magic back into the marriage." She headed for the door, Mark in tow. "Aren't you consumed by jealousy, raw jealousy?" she tossed over her shoulder.

"Naturally. You're a foxy lady, Catherine, even if you are old enough to remember the foxtrot."

She laughed loudly. "And the rumba. Watch me shake my stretch marks." With one hand pressed flat against her abdomen, the other in the air at right angles to her body, she danced a few steps, while Mark stood looking nonplussed. At the doorway she stopped and flung herself across the room at me one more time. "Geoffry Chadwick! You old sonofabitch!"

This time her embrace was frankly sexual, as she pressed her body against mine so that we fitted together like two halves of an indenture, curve flowing into curve, plane flat against plane. Then, embarrassed, she pulled away and went quickly up the stairs. Without words, she had just told me she loved me. And I found myself affected more than I cared to admit.

Mark stood at the foot of the stairs, one hand on the newel post. We smiled at one another.

"Duty calls," I said. "Up you go. As the immortal Robbie Burns once said: The best planned lays of mice and men, and so forth."

A look of such desolation crossed his face that I was immediately swept with regret. "Sorry, Mark, that was a cheap shot."

He went up to the landing. Framed by the large fan-shaped window, he paused and turned to look at me. " 'Why, there's a wench! Come on and kiss me, Kate,' " he said wryly.

I made a small bow. "I'll close up the house."

I turned off the lights in the living room, pulled the door onto the porch shut, and turned the handle which shot bolts into lintel and floor. The kitchen stood empty, the young lovers having retired to their *nid d'amour* over the garage. I stood looking into the refrigerator while cold air flowed softly over my feet, and decided on a piece of dry cheddar, which I chewed while getting undressed in my bedroom. Upstairs Catherine was, I hoped, enjoying whatever Mark had intended for me.

Without even bothering to wash my face or brush my teeth I eased myself into bed and, overcome with a sudden fatigue, fell asleep almost instantly.

XV

The following morning I opened my eyes gingerly. Mindful of having gone to bed with little in my stomach besides scotch, I fully expected reality to burst upon me clad in a headache and a mouth full of moss. To my astonishment, I felt all right, downright healthy; moreover I wanted to get up. As I swung my feet onto the floor I was conscious of more than ordinary stiffness across my shoulders and down my back and legs. But the soreness sprang from honest toil, as my father might have said; the mild discomfort was almost like a merit badge, worn with a self-conscious lack of self-consciousness.

I showered, scraped my face, scrubbed my teeth, scored my scalp with a comb. After pulling on the same clothes I had tossed onto a chair last night I strode into the deserted kitchen.

Catherine's coffeemaker seemed to have two or three pieces more than it really needed. While silently lamenting the passage of the percolator, I plugged in the electric kettle and set about finding a jar of instant coffee which, like soft-core porn, is no substitute for the real thing but better than nothing at all.

I felt ravenous, which was not surprising considering I had not eaten a real meal since Friday night's roast lamb. I tried not to dwell on how long ago that had been, all part of that mildly boring, uncomplicated evening when the country had seemed a sort of bargain basement Eden.

In the middle of pan scrambling eggs I looked up just in time to see Catherine limp down the hall. She looked, to use an old expression, as though she had been pulled through the wringer backwards.

"Good morning, Mary Sunshine," I sang out. "I have to admit you don't look the way Scarlet O'Hara did the morning after Rhett Butler carried her up the staircase."

"I'll just bet. And frankly, my dear, I don't give a damn."

"I couldn't figure out the combination for the coffeemaker. My first reaction was to smash it. I think I'm a closet Luddite. Would you like instant?"

"I'll cope." Catherine dealt with the machine. She sat at the kitchen table, neither asleep nor awake, a creature in a trance.

"How do you feel?" I asked suicidally.

"Do you even have to ask? I know I drank a bit last night, but not enough to make me feel the way I do."

"You have to admit yesterday was quite a day. You are hung over from far more than just drink. Believe me. Are you going to call the hospital. Or would you like me to?"

"I already did. Father is just the same. As soon as I get myself pulled together I'll go into town."

"I'll go along with you and look in on Larry. By the way, Madge said she wanted to know anything, at any time."

"I called her too. She was just on her way to the hospital."

"Did Mark tell you the Walfords took your car? And Madge has borrowed Larry's."

Catherine nodded just as Mark loomed in the doorway. This morning he looked his age.

"Good morning," I began. "Come and join the zombies. Want me to tell a couple of jokes?" I know that being cheerful in the morning around people who feel rotten just about defines cruelty, but the devil made me do it.

"Geoffry, people have been tarred and feathered for less."

By now the coffeemaker had stopped gargling and sputtering and micturating a stream of coffee into the glass pot.

"Let me pour for the first hour," I said, reaching down cups. "And what do we have on the agenda for the rest of the day?" I rubbed my hands together vigorously. "A country fair? Tea with the vicar? Yesterday is a tough act to follow."

"Deal with him, Catherine. He's your guest."

"He's your friend."

"Was."

As Catherine poured milk into her coffee I looked across the table at Mark and smiled. He returned the smile, then looked away. I knew then that we were going to be friends, that we both agreed last night was an episode better overlooked.

By the time we climbed into Mark's car for the trip to the hospital, my poisonous high spirits had been considerably dampened by the soggy aftermath of a large and unaccustomed breakfast. Having once seen a TV closeup of lions feeding it does not surprise me in the least that they sleep nearly twenty hours a day. I sat slumped in the back seat, wishing I were still in bed. Catherine had managed to conceal the ravages of the previous day under artful makeup. Mark had shaved; eliminating a day's growth of beard helped his appearance considerably.

There is something daunting about entering a hospital, even through the front door, and we walked single file into the building without speaking. Leaving Catherine and Mark to check on her father, I went directly to the room where Larry lay screened from three other occupants by a white curtain. Under-standably he looked grubby, lying there unshaved and uncombed on a battle-scarred hospital bed. In fact the entire hospital had the scrubbed but dented look of an institution whose budget does not permit new equipment.

"Good morning, Madame Ludmilla. I have in my possession a dubloon, also a Krugerrand. And you did offer to read my palm."

Larry smiled. "How do Pinocchio and his girlfriend make love?"

"I'd never guess."

"She sits on his face and he tells her lies." Larry laughed, then winced. "I'm not a well woman. But it only hurts when I frown. Aren't you going to sit on the edge of the bed and jiggle my shoulder?"

I moved to stand at the foot. "In a minute. How do you feel?"

"Better than I have any right to. I guess the sleeping pill took care of the hangover. My shoulder throbs. I'd sell my soul for a bloody mary. Other than that I'm fine."

"Where did you learn to handle firearms? I remember as a kid you weren't even allowed to play with my Daisy air-rifle."

"You have probably forgotten, but I'm just enough older than you to have spent six months in the service, at the very end of the war. Then Armistice, and I was discharged, honour-ably I might add. Which means they hadn't found me out. And they taught me how to shoot. Like riding a bicycle, it does come back."

"Had you planned all along to get the drop on Mikos?"

Larry shifted on the pillow, obviously trying to find a more comfortable position for his shoulder.

"Yes and no. I didn't have a specific strategy. And you know what I'm like on gin. I'd come on to Darth Vadar. He was definitely available. And I knew if I could isolate him and get those leather leotards down around his knees he could be taken. Coaxing him into the bathroom was a flash of pure inspiration."

"You could have been killed, or at least seriously wounded. As it is you lost a lot of blood."

"What do you want for nothing? I don't have to tell you that gin makes me a bit irrational. The more I thought about Catherine being kidnapped, the angrier I got. Sure, I made a lot of smartass remarks. But I was mad as hell underneath. Christ, Chadwick, you don't burst into a person's house and order the occupants around at gunpoint. Nobody enjoys being a victim better than I do, but on my own terms."

"Larry, I realize I am largely responsible for your being shot. I'm truly sorry. I acted without thinking, and my idea wasn't too swift. 'There's a trick with a pie I'm learning to do.' Believe me, I was afraid you might be killed."

"Chadwick, I've always said you're not a well woman. Why apologize? The lemon meringue caper probably saved my life. Even drunk as a skunk I don't think I could have pulled the trigger. I was hoping to bluff it out, but Four Eyes with the Howitzer wasn't about to be bluffed. Had you not acted, Mikos and I might both have been shot, like dead. I owe you one, several. You know, for someone who's really quite dreadful you're actually not bad."

Accolades of any sort, even disguised ones, have always made me uneasy. I cast about for something to say. "How will you get back to Toronto? Want me to drive you up in your car and fly back?"

"Thanks, but Madge has already offered. And she's going to stay with me for a bit. I'll need some looking after at first."

"She'll make one hell of a nurse."

"Won't she, though. Uniform by Yves St. Laurent, shoes by Capezzio, cap by Lily Daché, badge by Cartier."

We laughed, as old friends can laugh.

Larry shifted again. It was evident the shoulder was giving him quite a bit of action. "You said on the phone last week that you might be coming to Toronto. Did you mean it?"

"Yes, in a couple of weeks probably."

"Plan to stay an extra day, if you can. We can really tie one on."

"But, Larry, we always end up having a row when we get drunk together."

"And we always get over it. Please come."

Larry looked so depleted I felt a rush of something very like compassion. Having been the closest thing to perpetual motion I had encountered in my life, he now looked almost old. And to see Larry so slowed down was yet another mute but eloquent reminder of my own mortality.

"Sure I'll come, Larry. And if Madge has left I'll stay with you." That in itself was an enormous concession. Larry is never out of liquor. But he considers six eggs and a tin of sardines to be a well-stocked larder. And his house is an uneasy mixture of Bauhaus and Gustav Doré. "When are you going to be able to leave here and go back?"

"Tuesday probably. Madge wants to avoid the holiday week-end traffic. We may even break the trip in Kingston, if I can stand the excitement. When are you leaving?"

"I'll probably leave this afternoon, if I can pry my niece loose from the son of the house. I know I'm committed for the entire weekend, but I think Catherine and Mark have enough to contend with. And I'll probably have to drive out again to deal with the police. I'm sure Catherine will expect me to stay, so I'll give her a break and leave after lunch. Anything you want before I go?"

"Nothing, except a promise that you'll really come to Toronto."

"Larry, when a lady of my age and station gives her word." I reached over and took his left hand in mine. "I'll call."

"You know something, Chadwick? I thought this weekend was going to be dullsville, a real bummer. But I saw you and Mark and Catherine. I got taken hostage. I got drunk. I got shot. Madge and I became friends. Best of all, with my bum shoulder I have an iron-clad excuse not to attend that bo-ring sales conference on Tuesday morning. All things considered, I had a pretty good time."

"You can't beat the power of positive thinking." On the point of pushing aside the curtain, I turned. "By the way, when I get back to Montreal I'm going to be bad."

"How bad?"

"Marienbad."

"Ciao, Chadwick."

"Ciao."

I could tell Catherine was sorry as I announced my intended departure, but she did not press me to stay. To sit around for the next twenty-four hours playacting that nothing had really happened was far more than any of us could have pulled off. And she had all she could handle to get used to the idea of her father, whose condition promised a long siege of hospital, convalescence, daycare.

We ate our chicken salad and drank our white wine in the semi-silence of those preoccupied with their own thoughts. Even so, I was struck by the lack of constraint or self-consciousness. Unfortunate though they may have been, the events of the previous afternoon had bonded us. Like climbers who have survived a perilous expedition to the Himalayas or veterans of historic battles, we had undergone an experience which linked us together. Neither time nor absence nor distance could obliterate our sense of shared misfortune. We had become friends.

I had expected some opposition, at least a long face from my niece at the prospect of returning to Montreal after lunch; but she seemed perfectly amenable. The only person showing disappointment was Robert, committed to stay until the next day and reluctant to see his principal source of entertainment being taken away. Elizabeth excused herself to go and pack, the young man following, obviously bent on pushing his suggestion that she stay over and drive in with him on Monday afternoon.

"Catherine," I began, "what is the protocol regarding departing guests? Do I strip the bed and fold the sheets into tight little squares and stuff them into the pillowcases so you will have to separate and unfold everything before putting it into the washing machine?"

"While I am washing the car and splitting kindling? No, Geoffry, you are to do nothing at all."

"No guest book to sign?"

"No guest book. My dearest Geoffry, you have a grotesque and distorted concept of what country life is all about."

"I am an urban creature, Catherine. Next time people want to take me hostage, I want them to be announced by the doorman first."

"Very well. But be truthful. Can you honestly say you were bored?"

"No, I cannot."

"Did you even glimpse a spider?"

"No, I did not."

"You see! Now for the really big question. Will you ever come back again?"

"Yes, I will."

We all smiled, a bit self-consciously. High spirits are harder to fake than orgasm. I too went to pack.

An axiom for travellers. Clothes swell in inverse ratio to the space in which they were packed. As I forced the lid of my suitcase shut, I heard the telephone ring. When I carried my bag into the front hall, I saw Mark hang up the phone.

The caller, it turned out, was Madge. She had been listening to her radio on the way home from the hospital. Jean-Guy had been arrested on the Autoroute for running a toll booth without paying. The provincial police officer ordered him out of the car, and when Jean-Guy unfolded his skeletal height from behind the wheel he was recognized as one of the fugitives. Armed robbery, kidnapping, stealing a car, failing to stop when signalled by a provincial police officer, they all added up to a considerable shopping list of anti-social activities, enough to put him out of circulation for a while. By the time he was paroled he would be a middle-aged man with nothing to show for his life but years spent in jail. And all because he had been persuaded into joining an illegal get-rich-quick scheme by someone with far more drive and imagination. It is remotely possible that the meek shall inherit the earth, never the stupid.

I carried my bag outside, then pulled my car around to the

front door. Even as I stood waiting for Elizabeth I could feel the claustrophobia beginning to lift. Mark held the front door open for Catherine, and the two of them joined me by my car.

Catherine put her arms around my neck and laid her cheek against mine, not in the sexual way of last night, but as a mother might embrace a son. "I hate goodbyes," she sighed.

"So do I. But this is not goodbye. I'll be less than a hundred miles – God only knows how many kilometres – distant. And I may have to beg a bed if the local police want me to come back for further questioning. I'll telephone this evening, possibly a little bit tight, but still coherent. And I will see both of you when you bring your father to Montreal. We are undergoing at best a temporary separation."

I gave Catherine a bear hug, then released her.

"This wasn't quite the weekend I had planned," she said.

"Don't worry. But at least the events transpired to keep me out of the sailboat."

I grinned at Mark as I extended my hand to shake.

"Aren't you going to give Geoffry a hug?" demanded Catherine. "After all we've been through together?"

Only a little awkwardly, Mark and I put our arms around one another in that stiff, locker-room, back-slapping manner. He gave me a quick kiss on each cheek, as though he had just presented me with a medal in front of Napoleon's tomb. Then we separated, I suspect to our mutual relief.

I lifted the suitcase into the trunk of my car as Elizabeth came outside, virginal in a white mumu, her hair streaming down her back. At least I wasn't fooled. She and Robert had already said their own, I have no doubt tactile, farewells. There followed the usual exchange of thank you; it was lovely; come again soon. My niece and I got into the car and fastened our seat belts. I started the engine, gave a quick honk on my horn, and drove off. In the rear-view mirror I could see Mark and Catherine, arms around one another's shoulders, waving.

"You could have stayed over," I said to Elizabeth as we headed towards the Autoroute.

"I know that, Uncle Geoffry."

"I thought you liked Robert?"

"He's all right, I guess. But he was beginning to act as though he owned me. Fine, so we smoked a little grass and made it. That doesn't mean I want him to breathe for me."

"Will you be seeing him again?"

"Not deliberately. I may run into him, sure. But I won't be 'seeing' him again."

We drove in silence for a moment as I tried to remember whether I had packed my extra pair of glasses. Taking along two pairs of glasses on a weekend tells me something about myself I'd sooner not know.

"Uncle Geoffry, thanks for not making a big deal about Robert and me. I'd really hate Mother to find out. She's such a space cadet. She still talks about saving it for the right man."

"I know. Just as though he were going to arrive by courier, gift wrapped. What my sister does not realize is that if you want to turn a frog into a prince you have to kiss a lot of toads first. When I was young, your age, I kissed a lot of sleeping beauties and they never woke up. And to push this Grimm analysis to its illogical conclusion, just let me say this. There are a lot of wolves in the forest who will want to lift your little red riding hood and peek at your basket of goodies. But there won't always be a handsome woodcutter waiting in the wings. So be a little circumspect."

I pulled onto the Autoroute, bemused and perhaps a little bit saddened by my eighteen-year-old niece's lack of anything approaching surprise or wonder. When I was eighteen I thought getting laid was the greatest invention since the wheel. Maybe Mark was right. Maybe I was a closet romantic. But I couldn't help feeling just a bit sorry for someone who was so blasé and not yet twenty.

I smiled to myself as it occurred to me that Mark and I, then Catherine and I had, if only briefly, perhaps experienced more sexual communication than these two young people fucking away over the garage. And I can only speculate, but I suspect that both Mark and Catherine had surprised one another with the enthusiasm each had contributed to their conjugal coupling. Maybe innocence has to be learned, like guile. Children are not innocent, only inexperienced.

What would have happened had Elizabeth and Robert not interrupted Mark's and my wrestling match last night? I have a strong suspicion, but I did not want to think about the alternative at the moment. The important fact is that she did interrupt us and by her very presence prevented us from doing something, if not wrong, then perhaps foolish.

A totally unexpected surge of gratitude towards the young woman beside me who, albeit unwittingly, had helped two former lovers to become friends, caused me to smile broadly. Elizabeth caught my expression.

"What's so funny, Uncle Geoffry?"

"Oh, nothing, just a story I heard."

"Are you going to tell me?"

"It's not very interesting, really; something about a couple of mice, a town mouse and a country mouse who thought they would play while the cat was away."

"But that's a child's story, Uncle Geoffry."

"You're right, Elizabeth. It is."

XVI

other and I sat drinking quietly in the lengthening twilight. I had come to her apartment after putting Elizabeth on the Sunday late-afternoon train to Toronto. In just a few months she would be returning to Montreal to study. I did not grieve over the temporary separation. Over our first drink I had filled Mother in on yesterday's events, as much as I thought she needed to know. The story underwent some judicious editing.

"I was worried Elizabeth would be bored in the country, with no one but grownups," began Mother after I had freshened her drink with three more ounces of Polish vodka, which she drinks in preference to Russian as a kind of statement. What that statement really is remains unclear, especially to Mother. "And you, too, Geoffry. Even as a child you disliked leaving the city. You used to say it was like being buried, and every day was Sunday in the country. I remember you practically had to be kidnapped up to the lake."

I found her choice of words unfortunate.

Mother took a swallow of her drink and continued. "Your father disliked the country. He always claimed cities were man's highest achievement. And he died as he had lived, in Westmount. Poor Craig."

When Mother begins to reminisce about Father she can go on for ever, like a Christmas gift subscription to a magazine which must be endlessly renewed. I brought the conversation back to her.

"Be honest, Mother, you hated the country, much more than I did. Even as a child I can remember you spent the summers looking anxious. You were always terrified of bats."

"I still am. Horrid little creatures. But look what happened; Elizabeth went off to that nice barbecue, and you were taken hostage. I'll bet you weren't bored for a second."

"I hate to disillusion you, Mother, but being taken hostage is not nearly so much fun as you may think."

Mother took another longshoreman swallow of vodka. "Well, you have to admit that no situation is perfect. And you do have a penchant for finding fault. But why do you suppose Elizabeth left so abruptly? You didn't tell her she had to go, did you, Geoffry?"

"No, Mother, I did not. I merely suggested she might be more comfortable on the Sunday afternoon train as there will be hordes of people travelling tomorrow."

"I see. But you will stay for supper. I asked Walter to drop by for a bite, but he has gone to Vermont for the weekend. I can't imagine why. I do wish he were here."

"He has friends there. Anyhow, tough luck, Mrs. Chadwick. It looks as though you are stuck with me, Westmount's most eligible bachelor."

"It really is high time you married again, dear. I worry about what will happen to you after I am gone. How is Catherine Bradford, by the way? I remember her as being such a charming girl. I always felt you should have married her. Goodness me, what time is it?"

"Nearly seven."

"My word! It's time for *Fraggle Rock*." Mother heaved herself to her feet. "I do hope the Fraggles have enough commonsense to stay out of the Gorgs' garden. Are you going to join me and watch?"

"In a minute, Mother."

I watched Mother limp from the room into the den where she kept the huge TV console, then carried my drink over to the window. The city lay in that shimmering limbo between dusk and dark, the street lights casting a glow instead of a glare. How I loved the sight. Soon the view from Catherine's porch would be disappearing into that black void which shrouds the country and forces one indoors.

I was glad to have come to Mother's tonight. She obviously missed Walter; their frequent evenings together are a welcome part of the routine she dislikes having disrupted. What better bulwark against growing old than friends, I thought. I had watched Mother and Walter sustain one another over the years. She provided meals; he provided gossip. They were an oddly matched pair, but inseparable. Larry and Madge had obviously formed a bond; her being in Toronto was certainly going to help him over an awkward time. And I myself had just discovered, or rediscovered, two people who would make my life easier to inhabit. Maybe the weekend hadn't been such a write-off after all.

I stood looking out the window towards the St. Lawrence River, which I am certain Mother has not noticed once during the last five years. I realized with relief that Mark and I had exorcised old ghosts. Whatever happened in the future, we had left the past intact. I thought of Chris: exasperation recollected in tranquility. Who knows? Maybe one of these days he would get his act together. We might even grow to be real friends and cut ourselves loose from an old affair which seemed to drag along behind us like a U-Haul. I would like to think it might happen. We never really free ourselves from people who have touched our lives. It seems somehow more economical to incorporate them.

After I had watched Mother's program with her I would telephone Catherine and Mark. I had nothing in particular to say, nothing and everything. From where I stood I could hear the theme song of *Fraggle Rock*.

Carrying my drink, I went to join Mother in the den.

About one week later I was sitting in my office when Gladys Walker sashayed in with the mail.

"Would you like some coffee, Mr. Chadwick?" Without appearing to move she did something with her upper arms that made her breasts twitch.

"Not at the moment, thank you, Miss Walker."

She put the letters onto my desk and gonged her way out.

I picked up the top envelope and tapped it against my left thumb. Only yesterday Mark phoned to tell me that Mikos had been picked up in Sherbrooke, a small city some thirty miles or so from the lake. An alert policeman had spotted his leather drag, which he did not have the wit to discard. What cinched the identification was three gold studs in his left earlobe. For someone who didn't know how to row he was soon going to be heading up the river.

I presumed Leslie was still at large. Madge's orange Datsun had been found on a side street in the town near Catherine's house. The car was parked only a short distance from the bus station. Having abandoned the highly visible vehicle, Leslie probably took the first bus out of town. After discarding the mirrored glasses and possibly reversing his windbreaker he would have seemed like any other young man carrying a packsack and travelling on the holiday weekend. And in spite of all he had put us through during those tense and frightening hours, I still hoped he would not get caught. I knew I should think otherwise; but my subversive self, that part of me which dislikes hand-knitted socks and jars of home-made marmalade with bits of gingham covering the lid, silently cheered him on.

I turned my attention to the envelope at hand, postmarked Toronto, a plain white business envelope on which my name and the address of my office had been typed. There was no return address, either in the upper left-hand corner or on the back flap. I slit the envelope with my letter opener, a miniature damascene rapier from Toledo, and slid out a page which looked as if it had been torn from a magazine. It carried an advertisement for a popular make of flour; on a pedestal plate sat a lemon meringue pie in living colour. The ad promised pie crust of ethereal lightness were one to use this particular brand of flour. Across the top of the page was typed: "From pie in the eye to pie in the sky." Then beneath the picture a bit of doggerel had been written in ballpoint pen.

>   *I hope we meet again some day.*
>   *If not, I'm the one who got away.*
>   *(So it doesn't scan. Are you going to report me?)*

I found myself laughing out loud as I dropped the page and the envelope into my waste-paper basket. Then, still chuckling, I reached over and plucked the message from the basket to slide under my blotter. Face it; it's not every day that a man of my age receives a love letter.